SAMIRAH'S RIDE

THE STORY OF AN
ARABIAN FILLY

Annie Wedekind

Feiwel and Friends · New York

For Miriam

A Feiwel and Friends Book
An Imprint of Macmillan

samirah's ride. Copyright © 2010 by Annie Wedekind. All rights reserved.
Distributed in Canada by H.B. Fenn and Company Ltd. Printed in
May 2010 in the United States of America by World Color Press Inc.,
Fairfield, Pennsylvania. For information, address Feiwel and Friends,
175 Fifth Avenue, New York, N.Y. 10010.

Library of Congress Cataloging-in-Publication Data Available

ISBN: 978-0-312-38425-8

Book design by Barbara Grzeslo

Feiwel and Friends logo designed by Filomena Tuosto

First Edition: 2010

10 9 8 7 6 5 4 3 2 1

www.feiwelandfriends.com

Dear Reader,

Welcome to the Breyer Horse Collection book series!

When I was a young girl, I was not able to have a horse of my own. So, while I dreamed of having my own horse one day, I read every book about horses that I could find, filled my room with Breyer model horses, and took riding lessons.

Today, I'm lucky enough to work at Breyer, a company that is known for making authentic and realistic portrait models of horse heroes, great champions, and of course, horses in literature. This beautiful new fiction series is near to my heart because it is about horses whose memorable stories will take their place alongside the horse books that I loved as a child.

This series celebrates popular horse breeds that everyone loves. In each book, you'll get to appreciate the unique characteristics of a different breed, understand their history, and experience their life through their eyes. I believe that you'll love these books as much as I do, and that the horse heroes you meet in them will be your friends for life.

Enjoy them all!

Stephanie Macejko
Breyer Animal Creations

When Allah willed to create the horse, He said to the south wind:

"I will that a creature should proceed from thee—condense thyself!"—and the wind condensed itself. Then came the Angel Gabriel, and he took a handful of this matter and presented it to Allah, who formed of it a dark chestnut horse, saying:

"I have called thee horse; I have created thee Arab, and I have bestowed upon thee the color koummite. I have attached good fortune to the hair that falls between thy eyes. Thou shalt be the lord of all other animals. Men shall follow thee wherever thou goest. Good for pursuit as for flight, thou shalt fly without wings. Upon thy back shall riches repose, and through thy means shall wealth come."

–Letter of the Emir Abd-El-Kader,
from *Horses of the Sahara,* by E. Daumas

CHAPTER 1

Full of fire and full of bone,
All his line of fathers known

M Y NAME IS SAMIRAH—SAMI FOR SHORT, since I live on a ranch where almost everyone acquires a nickname. My old master came into this world as Jedediah Munk, and will leave it as Red. His wife, Mrs. Gloria Munk, is Miz M. Among her employees are a bearded, burly hand called Peach and a weedy fellow known as Bull. Even regular visitors get nicknamed: My farrier, April, is always called May, and the vet, Dr. McGowan, answers to Doolittle.

One of the few people called by her proper name is my companion, Jasper Munk, age twelve. Perhaps it's because she has an unusual name for a girl—almost like a nickname and a real name rolled into one. Or perhaps it's because she's known to kick, hard, if called anything else. "Freckles," "Pumpkin," "Carrot," "Slim"—all have been tried and all have painfully failed.

So I am Sami, Arabian mare, companion to Jasper, and member of the herd at the Cold Creek Ranch.

I was three years old when Red purchased me as a birthday gift for his then nine-year-old daughter and only child, Jasper. I was (and am) considered quite clever, so although at age three I was only halter-broke, Red decided that I would be a suitable friend to keep his daughter company.

"Both smart. Both redheads. Help me keep her out of trouble, won't you, Sami?"

I promised to try, and Red palmed me a carrot. Though he demanded much, Red had a generous spirit—like the rest of his family, as I was soon to discover.

I had an immediate affinity with Jasper—or she with me. After our many adventures together, it's difficult to know how much of her has been formed by me and how much of me has been molded by her. But, in the very beginning, her heart spoke to me as readily and as clearly as her voice and her hands, and both of these greeted me as if we had long been friends. And—who knows?—perhaps we always have been. I'm a great believer in destiny and history, as is Jasper, and perhaps we share a destiny, as much as we share a history.

"Is she mine? Is she mine?" the small girl cried as I

stepped off the trailer on that warm spring day, and her soft hands flickered over my coat, my mane, returning over and over to my muzzle.

"I think it might be the other way around," Miz M said, and Red laughed.

Yes, I'm yours, I thought. She was so particular, so different, and yet familiar despite her strangeness. We were both very young creatures, after all. Jasper, at nine, was her future self in miniature: slender and supple as a new blade of grass, with a tangle of hair almost the exact shade of dark red as my coat and clear gray eyes shining from her riotously freckled face. She was the smallest and the newest human I had ever met, and her fillyish excitement was infectious. My hooves danced in time with her skipping boots, and I breathed in her warm, flowery scent of the open fields where she played.

"Look at her nose, Daddy!" Jasper cried. "Look how big she's breathing!"

"That's why they call Arabians 'Drinkers of the Wind,'" Red told her. "Those big nostrils help them run fast, and to take in the world."

"She's going to run fast?" Jasper whispered. "Really fast?" Her feet went still, as did her hands. She stared up at me with fierce concentration.

"Oh yes," Red said. "But not just yet—at least, not with you aboard, Jasper. Sami's just a filly, and she's got a lot of learning to do. As do you, young lady."

And so it was that Jasper and I began our mutual education.

. . .

COLD CREEK RANCH IS PERCHED ON A GENTLE bluff overlooking the Green River, in the northeastern part of the state of Utah. The barn is very old but has become more solid and substantial with age, as if all the years of careful cleaning have polished it to a deep, mellow shine. (I suppose the same could be said for the main house, but I've never been in it.)

There was so much to see, to smell, and to listen to during the first days when I settled into my new home. Jasper was my primary guide, but I learned a great deal from the ranch's other humans and, eventually, even more from its horses. I soon struck up a friendship with Chief, a sturdy bay quarter horse who is ridden by the cowboy Peach. Chief was as easygoing and companionable as his rider—and much less intimidating than Cold Creek Ranch's lead mare, Magpie. With her glossy black-and-white coat and long, sweeping tail, Red's companion does indeed resemble the bird that is her namesake. She rules the herd with a benevolent despotism that, as a young filly, I did not fully appreciate. Almost as soon as we met, our wills clashed.

I am the daughter of a lead mare. My gentle mother, Sola, brightly colored, spirited, and swift as flame, governed the small herd in which I grew up. Her manner of leading and Magpie's were quite different, I soon found. Or perhaps I should say that life as the daughter of a lead mare and life as a young outsider were quite different.

I spent my first three days at the ranch in a roomy paddock near the barn. There was a bit of grass for grazing, and Jasper brought me a daily ration of hay and oats, as well as kept the drinking trough fresh. The paddock was an excellent vantage point for observing the workings of the ranch. In the morning, I watched the herd gather near the gate in answer to Peach's low whistle; then each horse was hitched to a post while Peach, Bull, and Jasper brushed the mud from their legs, picked hooves, and untangled manes and tails. Jasper had a little blue bucket she stood on to reach the taller horses. I'm afraid she wasn't much use to the ranch hands those mornings, for she was always skipping over to my paddock to make sure I didn't feel left out. There was hardly any muck, or room to muck about, in my pen, but she gave me a thorough polishing and combing each morning—I don't think I've been so clean since.

After the grooming, the horses were saddled and bridled. I was quite impressed with how workmanlike the herd seemed—quietly taking the bits, looking about them with interest, flickering an ear back to the people as they discussed the day ahead.

"Me and Chief will move the cows to the south pasture," Peach told Bull. "You get the trail ride, Bull, and Jasper, Miz M needs you in the house."

Jasper, unlike the horses, did not take this quietly.

"Aw, Peach, no! I need to lead Sami around and show her the creek and the best spots for drinking, and the view from the big hill, and her stall where I put up her new halter, and—"

Peach was grimacing in a way that looked entirely sympathetic to Jasper and wishing he had different orders for her, but just then her mother's voice sailed down from the kitchen window: "Jasper Munk! I need you as soon as you finish with the horses. We've got more guests coming tomorrow and beds to make and bread to bake and bathrooms to clean. Sami's tour can wait till after lunch."

Jasper's face was pink with fury and she kicked the hitching post so hard that Chief snorted an admonishment.

"I *hate* guests," she muttered. "Wish we were still a *real* ranch. Dumb old city slickers who don't know a thing about horses. Dumb old *cooking* and *laundry*... like I'm a maid instead of a *cowgirl*..."

Much of this was lost on me at the time, but as Jasper stalked toward the house, misery written in every small, tense muscle, I whinnied to her. She stopped, turned, and pelted back to me like a tiny foal to its mother. She flung her arms around my neck, swore to come back as soon as her chores were finished, and seemed in a slightly better humor after petting me about two dozen times.

· · ·

IN THE DAYS THAT FOLLOWED, AS JASPER AND I took long walks over the property, I learned what my companion had meant when she longed for a "real" ranch. I suppose I had been brought up on such a place, where raising horses and cattle were the humans' livelihood. And the Cold Creek itself had once been a thriving cattle outfit, according to Jasper, who was as proud of her family's history—her heritage—as I am of mine.

My family comes from the central Arabian desert–
bred by Bedouins to be strong, fast, hardy, and loyal to
our human companions. My ancestors were the nomadic
tribesmen's wealth and pride, and valued members of
their families. My mother and my grandmother told
me stories of the legends from our distant past, much as
Jasper's father instilled in her a pride of place. For me,
the place is not the source of pride–it's the blood of the
Arabian that flows through my veins. That, I can take
with me.

But I am getting ahead of myself. These are lessons I
tried to teach Jasper, in my own way. When she thought
she had lost her home, she felt she lost everything. The
Arabian has long known that home is where your herd
is, where your family is, and that, as we learn during
our far-flung and well-traveled lives, can be anywhere.

But Cold Creek Ranch was Jasper's home, and perhaps the waters of the Green River flowed in her veins.
This was a majestic and noble land–I sensed that from
the moment my hoof first touched down from the trailer
and I inhaled the lush, fresh fragrance of well-watered
grassland, the pink-and-white-flowering salt cedar trees,
and the pungent aroma of sage and greasewood. Far
from any town, nestled near the banks of the great river,

and cupped in the foothills of a series of rocky moun-
tainsides, the ranch was almost as ageless as my ances-
tral desert sands. During my early days in the corral, I
yearned to run those fields, to drink from the river, even
to explore the mountain ranges. I fear I was as difficult
to contain as Jasper, though I tried to remember my
training and to be patient.

The first walks that Jasper and I took satisfied some
of our need to be free. Red decided I should "settle in"
for a few days (hence the corral) before I was introduced
to the herd (he couldn't have known that these introduc-
tions were performed the same day I arrived, though
from a distance), so Jasper and I were alone in our ex-
plorations. She showed me the pasture where I would
live, the shady banks of the two streams that branched
out of the river, let me sniff over the ranch's buildings,
from the horse barn to the cattle shed, the flourishing
vegetable garden just outside the kitchen of the main
house, and even showed me the remains of her ancestors' original dwelling—a curious little house like an
animal's cave, built directly into the side of a rounded
slope, with earth and grass as its roof. In their long-gone
century, the ranch had been, to Jasper's mind, "real":
Those first Munks had raised their cattle, their horses,

built a ferry to cross the river, even established a store to serve the needs of this small pioneer outpost. Now, of course, it was all different.

"It's the guests," Jasper explained to me on an early walk. "After Grandpa died, Dad decided we could only keep the ranch going if we took in tourists. So he built those cabins"—here she pointed out a series of neat, small lodgings scattered some distance from the house—"and basically turned everything into a hotel or something. But like a hotel with activities—you know, fishing, riding, playing cowboy with the poor old cows. It's just . . . *silly.*"

I was reminded of a relative on my father's side—an unusually tall gray—who had been sold to the circus. He spent his days pretending to be a wild stallion—he was, in fact, a gelding—who was "tamed" by a series of stunt riders who jumped around on his back like frogs. I snorted sympathetically. A horse knows about the human fondness for playacting.

"The worst thing is all the chores," Jasper went on. "My mom treats me like a *servant* when we have guests. And Dad and Peach always tell me to mind her. I don't mind helping—really—I just *hate* helping in the house. Wish we could get somebody else to do it. Wish I could just help outside and in the barn. Dad says when I'm older . . ."

Here she paused and lay her small cheek against my shoulder, her right hand reaching up to twist her fingers through my mane. I sighed, relishing the feel of the warm June sun on my coat, drinking in the tantalizing smell of the grass. I lowered my head to graze, and Jasper let me, sinking down herself and inserting a blade of grass between her teeth.

"Jasper, you watch that filly doesn't step on you, now," came Bull's reedy voice from behind us. "It ain't safe to lie down on the ground with an unbroke horse on top of you."

"Don't be silly, Bull," she reprimanded. "Sami would *never* step on me."

Indeed not. I shot a cool glance at the ranch hand and made a point of lifting my hooves prettily as I moved to a new, tufty patch. Red had brought me to Cold Creek to be Jasper's horse, and no Arabian worth her blood would take that responsibility lightly. I was spirited, young, flightier than I am now, but never unaware of my human companion and my duty to her. Yes, I longed to run free over those beautiful meadows, longed to fully meet the herd that I was to join, but while I was tethered to Jasper by my halter and lead rope, I would be patient, calm, and well mannered. Anything less would be a betrayal of my heritage.

Arabians are often accused of pride, but I don't think that it's a fault unless combined with arrogance or bullying. I am proud of my bloodlines, and I am proud of myself—I feel in the soundness of my stride, the high carriage of my tail, the coiled energy in my quarters, the impress of the ages. Even my color, *koummite*, or blood bay, is the shade of the First Horse. I was made to carry prophets and kings, warriors and raiders. And Jasper.

CHAPTER 2

Give the preference to mares; their belly is a treasure, and their back a seat of honor

---

AFTER THREE DAYS IN THE CORRAL–comfortable, but confining–I finally got to join the herd.

That morning it was Red, not Jasper, who came to fetch me, though of course Jasper shadowed his heels and had lots of instructions for how to handle me, to which her father lent a tolerant ear. She showed him how I liked to eat my carrots (tip up, not lying in the palm), but I wasn't very interested in the treat. I could sense that today was different. Not only was the morning routine changed, with Red's hand at my halter, but I felt a watchfulness and a certain tension from the herd just beyond the double line of the corral and pasture's fences.

I said that the herd and I had already introduced ourselves from afar–that is, we caught one another's scent and neighed back and forth to confirm their possession of the territory and my status as an outsider. I expected this.

My mother had told me that as a newcomer, and a young filly, I would not have the same rank as I held in my old herd as cherished daughter of a respected lead mare. I was both eager to fully meet the other horses and wary.

As Jasper opened the corral's gate and Red led me through, I couldn't contain the excitement and nervous energy that rippled through my body. All of my senses were keyed to their highest, my ears strained forward so that the tips nearly met in the middle, and I pranced in place.

"Steady on, girl," Red said, his gravelly voice as reassuring and calm as ever.

"She's excited, isn't she, Dad?" Jasper smiled up at both of us.

"Just like you on the first day of school." Red chuckled. "To her, all these horses are like new boys and girls to meet. Well, guess Magpie'd be the teacher."

"You don't think she'll pick on Sami, do you, Dad?"

"Horses have their own way of sorting themselves out. What's important for them is knowing where they stand in the group. An outsider shakes them up, so it can be a little rough for everybody at first."

"Especially for the new girl." Jasper reached around her father to pat my flank.

"Don't worry, Jasper. Magpie will keep everybody straight. And I think Chief already has a crush on Sami, don't you? All the other horses like him, so if he takes to her, that'll help."

As they talked, Red unlatched the pasture gate. It was Sunday—the herd's day of rest—and everyone had been fed. I was the only object of interest, and as I felt all of the strange eyes examining me, I suddenly had an urge to bolt. But where to? I was no longer a member of my mother's herd. This was my home now. I arched my neck, flared my nostrils, and gave a brief whinny . . . but I'm afraid it was of challenge, not of supplication. Immediately, I saw the ears of the black-and-white mare at the forefront of the group swivel backward. Magpie was not pleased by my brief declaration of independence.

I took a closer look at my new leader. Magpie was a well-muscled, powerful pinto mare who, despite her average size, always carried Red effortlessly. I already knew he doted on her, in his own way, almost as much as Jasper fussed over me. She was his only mount. I had watched them together and been impressed by their harmony of purpose, the near-seamless meshing of cue and response, a task set and its fulfillment. I had seen horses and humans working together my whole life—all three years of it—but, having yet to be ridden, it still seemed strange to me how the partnership was achieved. I told myself it didn't frighten me—especially since the human I would eventually carry would be Jasper—but it was still an unexperienced mystery, this conjoining of horse and person. And it was one that Magpie knew and practiced to its utmost. *I must respect her,* I thought. Another part of me protested: *But I am Sola's daughter!*

Magpie's ears remained pinned as Red closed the gate behind us. Her white markings covered half her face—an outsize blaze—so one light blue eye examined me from a background of glossy black, the other from snowy white. I had never seen such markings before, but my admiration was dampened by the imperious, annoyed expression the colors framed.

"An Arabian," the pinto snorted. "Get away from here. We're watering."

I froze. We hadn't even sniffed each other yet! I still had my halter on! Red was standing right next to us, and she was ordering me away!

Red told Jasper to stay outside the pasture, so she found a perch on the lowest slat of the fence to watch the meeting. As I faced the herd, I wished that she was by my side.

Red unbuckled the halter and eased it from my head, murmuring gentle reassurances and stroking my neck. Then he stepped away from me, toward Magpie. He gave her a carrot from his pocket and ran an affectionate hand down her crest.

"Here's Sami, old girl. Show her the ropes and don't let the other horses bully her too much. She's young, like you were once." And with those words, Red opened the pasture gate and went out. The rattling of the chain as he secured the fence made me jump.

From the look on Magpie's face, Red's words had had little effect on her opinion of me. Her ears were still swiveled back and she swished her long black tail in a marked manner. I took a sideways stride, away from her, but I was hemmed in by the rest of the herd, who regarded me with a not-unfriendly curiosity.

"Hullo, Sami." Chief nodded. He was a tall, stocky bay with a big head and almost comically large ears that gave his homely face an innocent expression. I breathed in his scent—earthy, warm, and quite male— and nickered an acknowledgment of his greeting. The other horses—seven in all, plus Magpie and Chief— seemed to want to approach, but as I watched them glance between me and the lead mare, I knew that they were cautious of moving forward without Magpie's approval.

When you become acquainted with the lead mare, your position within the herd will fall naturally into place. The other horses will take their cue from her.

My mother was certainly right about that, but she hadn't said anything about what to do if the lead mare didn't like me!

Magpie must have sensed that the herd was awaiting her next move. With a short, high blast—more explosion than whinny—she again commanded me to stay away from the water trough. Well, I wasn't thirsty, anyway. I took another crab step and eased around the edge of the group, keeping my distance from the horse closest to me, a dun mustang who was ridden by Miz M. From my paddock, I had watched this horse—called Buck—with interest. There was something not quite trained about him, an energy that I responded to. I wanted to make his acquaintance, but this did not seem to be the moment.

"Go!" Magpie blasted again, and this time she snaked her neck toward me in a way that clearly added, *Or I will bite you!* Now I was afraid. I bolted away from the herd. I could hear Jasper's dismayed voice behind me as I cantered toward the hills:

"Magpie chased her off! How mean!"

I couldn't have agreed more. As I slowed my strides and looked back toward the other horses taking turns at the trough (Magpie, of course, was first), I suddenly felt very lonely. The pasture was large, the grass abundant, the view splendid—but unless I gained a place with my new family, I could not enjoy it.

I was very young then, but I can still remember the ache I felt as I watched the other horses swishing flies and grazing companionably together. Only Magpie held herself apart, her eyes fixed on me. We both stood like that for a long time.

. . .

THE FIRST WEEK WAS TERRIBLE. I FELT LIKE AN outcast—I *was* an outcast—and I quite simply had no idea what to do about it. I spent my days moping along the most distant edge of the herd's range. I watered at the far-off creek, not the trough, and I couldn't bring myself to go near the common food buckets. Luckily the grass was more than enough for my needs; after all, I wasn't working like the others and had no real appetite for oats.

Everyone was working now, humans and horses alike. In my solitary rambles, I watched the arrival of the guests that Jasper had dreaded—one older pair and one family with two children. They moved into two of the cottages and soon Chief and Peach were leading trail rides, Red was heading fishing expeditions, and Bull was helping the young boys learn how to sit a horse. Jasper and Miz M seemed swallowed up by the main house. During the day, I caught glimpses of Jasper gathering vegetables from the kitchen garden and cleaning tack in the shade of the barn. The expression on her small, usually dirty face looked as miserable as I felt. She visited me early in the morning before starting her chores, and at night after sunset. She had (and still has) a special whistle that she used to call me—a long, high note followed by three short, lower notes—and once I learned that that birdlike song meant Jasper, companionship, and carrots, my spirits lifted as soon as I heard it. Those notes cut through my loneliness like a sunbeam.

We consoled each other during those confidential sessions by the fence. Sometimes we stood in silence, Jasper gazing upward at the stars while I breathed in the evening air, fragrant with juniper and sweet anise. Those nights, my whole being was filled to the brim. During the day, lonely and with nothing else to occupy me, I often released my frustrations by running, especially when the herd was taken out to be saddled for work. As they were led through the gate one by one, I would gallop the fence line, whinnying to Chief, even to Buck, willing my body forward, faster and faster in a display of . . . I don't know what. All I knew was that running eased the pressure around my heart. They watched me when I ran, humans and horses alike, and if Jasper was outside to see me, she cheered and clapped and jumped up and down like a grasshopper. Drinking the air, stretching my legs farther and farther, feeling the blood surge through me—I was, in those moments, free.

But a horse needs a herd. Room to run, carrots, wind clear and cool as river water—none of these things can make up for not having a place with other horses. The only thing that came close was Jasper, and perhaps that's another reason why we've always been so bound up together. For a while, *she* was my herd.

As the days passed, I spent less time moping and more time watching the other horses. The herd was a mix of geldings and mares, which took some getting used to. (My mother's herd was only mares—the stallions and the geldings were kept in separate fields and had their own barns.) Besides Chief and Buck, there was an old palomino gelding named Sunny. The humans only used him for the easier trail rides, and the horses gave him a respect second only to that they showed Magpie. Wherever he went, he was sure to be shadowed by Cricket, a quiet chestnut mare with a white stripe and one white stocking, or Irish, a tall, graceful bay mare who, besides me, was the newest to the ranch and lowest in the pecking order. The last mare, Julep, was Magpie's second in command, and stuck to her like a burr.

Sunny, however, wasn't really the dominant gelding. He was beloved, and emulated, but he never tried to control the herd. That was Buck, who seemed to play stallion to Magpie's lead mare. Buck may be gentled, trained to carry Miz M and to be a respectful member of the Cold Creek family, but domestication had not diluted his mustang blood. Later on, after I'd gotten to know him better, I marveled at the small dun's keen senses and nose for danger. He seemed to have a heightened awareness of his surroundings, and a ferocious drive to protect the herd. This led to some run-ins with Magpie, who most decidedly did not see a cougar in every shadow or a potential lightning strike in every rainstorm. She accused him of nervousness; he thought of it as preparedness.

And then there was the Artful Dodger, who, if he'd been allowed, would have taken over the whole operation and set himself up as king. I loved watching Dodger—it was my primary pleasure, outside of galloping and visiting with Jasper. He was a trim, perfectly proportioned black pony with four white socks, a face dished rather like my own, and a heart full of mischief. He constantly challenged both Magpie and Buck for precedence, but no one took him seriously. Indeed, they mostly indulged him as if he were a precocious colt, unless he went too far, as he did one evening after the herd, tired from a long day, was settling into its nighttime graze.

Dodger certainly had worked as much as everyone else—he had a lesson with one of the boy guests and had carried the other on a lengthy trail ride. Yet he trotted with a bossy little bounce straight over to Sunny, nipped the palomino's distinguished rump, and drove him away from Irish, with whom he'd been swishing flies. Sunny merely gazed mildly at his usurper, while Irish looked startled, but Magpie had seen the exchange, and Magpie disapproved. There was a scuffle, a small yelp-like neigh, and then Sunny and Irish were reunited and Dodger reappeared on the other side of the field, grazing unconcernedly. I admired that. Dodger was often down, but he was never out.

I suppose that it was only natural that the pony was

the first to break the prohibition against me. Chief, of course, always said hello, but from a distance. His attitude was clear: He liked me, looked forward to having me in the herd, but was perfectly content to wait for Magpie's directive. Buck's desires were, if anything, even more obvious. He took to standing on the crest of one of the many hills that framed the pastureland and trumpeting wildly to me. It translated best as *Mare! See what a fine horse I am! You are mine! Come!* Magpie ignored these outbursts, and so did I. As my mother once remarked, mares often suffer for the foolish things a stallion (or gelding) tells them to do without the lead mare's permission. They are simply too addled by the sense of their own wonderfulness to appreciate consequences.

Dodger, really, was no better. He was just cleverer. It was Sunday, a week since I'd been let into the main pasture, and I was standing in the creek, swishing flies by myself, and staring into the green tangle of willow and fern that framed the banks. Suddenly I noticed two bright brown eyes peering at me through the branches. The low eye level, the insouciant sparkle, the bold gaze—it could only be Dodger. It had been so long since I'd had any significant contact with another horse, I'm afraid I was rather at a loss. Chastening to admit, spirited and independent as I've always fancied myself, how low I had been brought by Magpie's banishment.

"Chase me?" was all that Dodger said. And he promptly turned tail and slipped between the trees. I automatically took a few steps forward, but then stopped. It could be a trick. Dodger could be trying to tempt me out to get me in trouble. I was standing indecisively, my front legs on the bank, my back hooves still in the creek, when I heard approaching hoofbeats.

"Bet I can beat you," the pony chirruped.

That was simply too much.

I leaped from the creek bed, eyes fixed on the small black hindquarters weaving with Dodger's characteristic springy gait through the trunks. *Pony, you are no match for an Arabian,* I thought. He had the advantage in the woods, being smaller and more familiar with the trails, and I plunged through the foliage, eager to reach the great open field where I could run freely.

Finally I was through the last of the trees. But where was Dodger? I pulled myself up, looking confusedly right and left. Surely he hadn't managed to put *that* much distance between us. Was this indeed a trick?

The nip on my flank confirmed it. I startled violently,

but when I turned to meet my foe, I saw that merry face laughing at me.

"Catch me if you can!" And away Dodger went.

Of course he couldn't beat me, and I'm not sure he really tried. I caught up with him easily and returned his nip. He stopped in his tracks and changed directions. I cut him off and we play-reared at each other. Over the hills, across the great expanse of rippling grass, we whirled and tagged and jostled and galloped. Finally even the seemingly inexhaustible Dodger grew tired, and he slowed to a jog. I cantered in circles around him, tossing my head, arching my neck, and teasing him to my heart's content. I felt wonderful. My muscles burned, my nostrils were open wide, and I had a friend by my side. We had *played*, and oh, I hadn't played for such a long time!

I was so caught up in our banter (*I'm faster! So? I'm smarter. Are not! Am too. Are not! Am too, and besides, now you're my mare. I'm nobody's mare! Are too. Am not!* etc.) that I wasn't paying much attention to which direction we were going. So when we reached the crest of one of the ranch's many low buttes, I immediately pulled up and snorted in surprise. There, standing to attention as if they were expecting us (and they probably did hear our noisy tussling), was the herd. No one was grazing. No one was swishing flies. Manes tousled in the breeze, an alert, wary expression on each face, the eight horses stood still as stones on the windy crest. My own body was not so perfectly controlled. I tossed my head, crab-stepped sideways, toward Dodger, and skittered nervously back and forth, more chicken than Arab. I wished then that I had Dodger's irresistible nonchalance—and I wonder now what it might be like to inhabit his funny, confident pony self. But I was a wild young creature, missing her mother, proud and frightened, not yet a full member of Jasper's world, and unwanted, it seemed, by the family that stood before me.

Dodger moved to join the other horses, leaving me alone once again. As he reached Irish, lifting his dainty head to touch muzzles with the tall bay filly, who towered several hands above him, Magpie turned; and the herd, on her signal, began to walk away from me. I watched them go, an aching sorrow once more binding up my heart, which had just beat so freely, running the hills with Dodger. When—if ever—would my sentence end?

And then, out of the blue, Magpie threw a glance over her shoulder at me. "Well, come on," she whinnied.

I stared back at her, shock rooting me in place. "If you won't keep up, we'll leave you behind," she promised crisply, as if I were a lollygagging foal.

I looked bewilderedly to Dodger, but he was still involved with Irish, taking advantage of her low position in the herd to play stallion, herding her into last place of the loose line of horses now making their way to the pasture's gate. It was Chief who answered my silent, unbelieving question.

"That's right, Sami girl," he snorted. "Come along now."

Relief and joy coursed through me with the warmth of the spring's first mellow sun, the one that gives true heat as well as light. I leaped forward, toward the herd, toward my family, to the place where I belonged. It was right behind Irish, making me the lowest and youngest and least important—and happiest—filly at Cold Creek Ranch.

CHAPTER 3

Her forelock is a net, her forehead a lamp lighted,
Illumining the tribe

———

YOU MIGHT SAY THAT WAS THE DAY I learned humility. But that would be too simple. Humility, after all, is not one of my notable traits. Nor is it one of Jasper's, and if we're still counting reasons why we're such good partners, that's another.

And, of course, we grew up together. As I mentioned, I was three and she was nine when we met. She was already a fine rider, Dodger and Cricket being her usual mounts, but I had had nothing heavier than a winter blanket on my back, and wouldn't for a couple more years. If Jasper and I are not known for humility, we're not exactly renowned for patience, either, but as much as she wanted to ride me, and as eager as I was to grow up, I wouldn't exchange a single moment from our early time together. It was the beginning of the games.

You might not think a horse has very much imagination, or historical sense, and I can't speak for every breed, but Arabians are highly developed in both areas. Perhaps it's a product of our close tie to humans, perhaps we're simply cleverer than most horses. I suspect both. Of course there are all sorts of ways for horses to be intelligent (and unintelligent). Buck, for example, had an uncanny instinct for sensing change—change of weather, of habitat, of human activity. This made him act on the twitchy side, when, say, his prediction of a dire storm turned out to be a gentle summer shower, or when the humans making alarming sounds along the pasture's fence line turned out to be repairing it, rather than plotting to tear a hole through the boards and steal the mares. Sunny and Magpie, on the other hand, were very intelligent about human communication, especially when being ridden. I suppose that had something to do with how strongly they both trusted all of the men and women of the ranch, much more so than any of the other horses. To be sure, we *all* trusted Red and Miz M and Peach and Bull, but Sunny and Magpie would calmly walk through a burning barn if commanded. There was something preternatural in their ability to suppress their flight instincts, to be almost *more than horse* for their human companions.

Magpie and Sunny were also herd leaders, so they were smart about equine communication, as was Dodger, who seemed to know exactly how much he could get away with. Some horses are deaf to the workings of a herd, and tend to make themselves unpopular and miserable as a result. I am thinking in particular of Zelda, a brown-and-white-patterned Appaloosa who was always uneasy about her place in the herd. She challenged Magpie for precedence, bullied the other mares, and generally made herself disagreeable. She didn't know where she belonged—she had been the second-ranked mare at the herd she lived in before Red brought her to the ranch—and she did her best to make the rest of us feel just as uncomfortable. Luckily, her best wasn't very much, and she was no match for Magpie. The only horse who really tolerated Zelda well was Chief, but then he wasn't known for his particularity. Chief, I'd discovered, was not terribly bright, but he did have a remarkable ability to form friendships, and he was utterly reliable.

Of course even a clever horse can have her wits dulled by a dull human, especially if the horse is sensitive. Rough handling, inconsistency, unnecessary correction: too-common human traits that first confuse, then frighten, then alienate a horse. Not every filly is lucky enough to belong to a human with the wisdom of Solomon (or, for that matter, to belong to King Solomon himself, like several of my ancestors who were imported from Egypt for his stables).

But I digress from my original point, which was about the games and how they factored into my early training. You might think that a nine-year-old girl is too young to be responsible for any serious horse training, but Jasper was her father's daughter, and her father taught her well. In between her chores (more onerous in the spring and summer months) and school (which took up quite a bit of her time in autumn and winter), Red trained Jasper to train me.

I was already accustomed to being handled and groomed and led. Soon I learned to walk in circles around Red, then Jasper, from a long lead they called a lunge line. From walking, halting, and changing directions, I progressed to trotting and cantering, having to pay close attention to when they wanted me to quicken or slow my pace, or to stop altogether. It required focus, and it made me a little dizzy, especially cantering (I'm quite fast). But soon Jasper found a way to make it fun.

The paddock became a racetrack, the sands of the Sahara, and a rodeo stadium, among other incarnations. I would be introduced in ringing tones as "Samirah! Amazing Arabian of the West!" Before our lessons,

Jasper would braid wildflowers in my mane, tail, and forelock, as Bedouins decorated the forelocks of my ancestors, and the repetition of this ritual thrilled me to the core. Peach joked that I turned into a princess when Jasper adorned me, far too proud and high-spirited for my own good. But for me, the flowers and ribbons were more than mere decoration—they crowned me, they honored the legend of my tribe, that fortune and happiness were bound up in, of all things, my very forelock. Princess? I rather think *queen* is more appropriate. Jasper's delight in my quickened gait, the proud arch of my neck, the high carriage of my tail, inspired me even more than the flowers. Oh, the riches of friendship! Jasper's love for me came in gifts of flowers, her love for my beauty made me want to be more beautiful still, and my response to her happiness made her, if possible, happier still. I was well on my way to trusting her, to wanting to do *everything* for her, as Sunny and Magpie did for the rest of her family. I was learning, and sometimes the lessons seemed incomprehensible, but never the lesson of love. That was written in Jasper's eyes, and in mine.

· · ·

"RIDICULOUS," ZELDA SNORTED AS I TROTTED over to the water trough. Jasper had just turned me out in the big pasture after our morning lesson, in which I'd perfected backing at Jasper's voice command. But I hadn't backed as Sami, Cold Creek Ranch horse. I'd backed as Sami, famed mount of a Native American scout (Jasper), who was training her horse to move silently and deftly through the sagebrush and nettles (never mind that the corral's footing was firmly packed dirt). Being an Indian pony, I had a bold white circle painted over my left eye and zigzagged stripes like streaks of lightning down my forelegs. I felt very fierce and brave.

I tossed my head and headed for the water trough. After bullying Julep one too many times, Zelda had recently been demoted (again) to lowest mare on the herd totem pole. This meant that I was promoted, however temporarily, and the Appaloosa was anything but pleased. I didn't have a great deal of sympathy for her—she made that difficult—but it did occur to me, as I put my head down and drank, that it might be lonely not being *somebody's* horse. Chief had Peach, Magpie had Red, Buck had Miz M, Julep had Bull, and Sunny sort of belonged to the entire family, but the rest of the horses were there for the guests, and when there weren't guests, they were rather at loose ends. It gave them more time to squabble for precedence and fret about little things like dinner not being exactly on time or having to be clipped. And maybe even Dodger would be less naughty if he had a young person to be his companion. Well, maybe.

At least the Artful Dodger was cheerful with his infractions. Zelda was just plain cranky, and Cricket moped a lot. Only Irish seemed thoroughly at peace with her haphazard riding schedule and periods of inactivity. As I raised my dripping muzzle and gave a little snort of satisfaction, I caught sight of the elegant bay, quietly staring out over the hills. I decided to see if she'd like to swish flies with me. I'd only done this with Chief and Dodger so far, but my promotion to second-lowest mare, and perhaps my Indian pony paint, gave me the courage to approach her.

I walked slowly up the grassy slope, giving Irish time to warn me away or to retreat if she was so inclined. But the mare didn't even seem to notice me until I was almost to her flank, and then she turned with startled eyes. I blew out what I hoped was a reassuring breath and nickered. Her expression softened and she sighed. I took this for encouragement and angled my body toward hers so my tail could reach her right shoulder. A moment later, she eased a step closer to me and I felt the flick of her tail near my withers. *How nice,* I thought.

She must have felt the same, because we stayed that way for quite a while, gazing out in opposite directions of the same green view. It was late summer and the birds were busy harvesting the serviceberry fruit. Buck could probably already scent the first hint of autumn on the warm breeze, but to me the ranch seemed garlanded with life. Perhaps this was the secret to Irish's peace, the richness of these hills, this place. Perhaps she had lived in a different sort of world before. My mother had told me that some horses did not have the luxury of space to roam, fields to graze. I couldn't imagine it, but something told me that Irish could—and had.

. . .

CHIEF WAS PLEASED THAT I'D MADE FRIENDS with Irish, and under his protective guidance, I soon was on good terms with the entire herd, excepting Zelda. Magpie still held herself aloof, but I felt I understood her better now, having watched her with Red. She considered herself his partner, and while she took her responsibilities with the herd seriously, I could tell that she felt that her true place was under Red's saddle. She seemed always to be waiting for his whistle, for the sound of his hand at the gate. Of course, I was getting to be the same way about Jasper.

When autumn came, the golden birch leaves dappled the creek like coins of sunlight and the sumac caught fire in hues that rivaled my coat. I liked to look at Jasper's tangled braid resting against my shoulder, to see the russet hair next to my own coppery shade, then to look up to the transformed trees, molten orange and apple red. Autumn suited us beautifully.

"You two under the maple tree make my eyes hurt!" Miz M laughingly complained. We were indeed the next brightest creatures to the flaming branches. True, my long mane and tail are black, as is my muzzle and the area around my eyes where the midnight skin of the Arabian is revealed, but it's a deep black that contains fire and velvet and the gleam of embers.

"I am Vulcan, god of Fire!" Jasper called back. "And this is my celestial steed!" I liked the sound of that.

"Does the celestial steed know that Vulcan needs to come inside and finish her homework?"

"Gods don't have homework!"

Unfortunately, Vulcan seemed to be the exception. That night, I looked up to Jasper's window, which faced the pasture, and watched her silhouette against the room's yellow glow. For a while, she appeared to be sitting very still, concentrating, her forehead resting on one hand. Then she shook herself, stood, and stretched out her arms.

"Vulcan has finished her homework!" she shouted out the window, and I could hear her mother's laughter from the kitchen window below. Jasper might want to be a rebel, but she was a very responsible one.

She reminded me so much of a filly. Her instincts and her duties intertwined, often tugging at each other. I must admit that sometimes when Jasper led me to the corral for training, even though I really did want to please her, and mostly enjoyed the work, part of me was also tempted to try to break free, to break for the mountains to see what they held, to goad Dodger into a game of chase, to hide down by the creek and be a very naughty, but free, filly. How many horses are lucky enough to have a companion who can sense this? Who can see the wild, untrained heart straining within the civilized form? I am fortunate to be one of them. On my untamed days, Jasper led me back out of the corral (oh, how my hooves danced when that gate closed behind us!) and took me for a walk instead.

Looking back, I realize that these walks were quite as educational as my groundwork, but it was the sort of learning that sinks in gently, through the skin rather than through the head. I was taught to follow Jasper through the creek and over the metal cattle guard that fronted the entrance to the ranch, though the clatter of my hooves over the strange, slippery surface made me shiver. I learned about the hazards of holes and poisonous plants in the pasture as Jasper filled the one and uprooted the other. And I heard a great deal more about the ranch's history.

"When I can ride you," Jasper told me, "we're going to visit Browns Hole and Robber's Roost, where Butch Cassidy kept his horses. I guess he knew a lot about horses, that's what Dad says. He was a real outlaw, Sami! Him and his gang . . . well, they were just about the best outlaws in the West, I think. I bet you didn't know you lived on the Outlaw Trail, huh? Well, it used to be. Now it's just for tourists, and us." Jasper sighed heavily. "I wish we could've lived then. When my great-great-grandfather first settled here and built Cold Creek. Talk about wild! It must have been just about the wildest place in the Wild West. . . ." Jasper's voice trailed off, but suddenly her breath quickened and her eyes sparkled.

"Oh, Sami! Can't you just see us! Jasper the Kid and Sami the . . . the . . . Red Blaze! No, that sounds weird. Sami the Sunburst? That makes you sound like a piece of candy. Hmm. Don't worry, I'll think up a great bandit horse name for you. Oooh—Bandit! Sami the Red Bandit! That's it!"

I suspected that we would be playing Outlaw for a long time. But I didn't know how deadly serious the game would become.

CHAPTER 4

Her stride swallows the distance
Yet her canter becomes a soft cushion.
She stands high over the earth . . .

———

"EASY . . . EASY . . . STEADY ON, GIRL . . . EASY! whoa!"

And for the third time that morning the saddle hit the earth with a *whump,* kicking up a cloud of dust that drifted upward like smoke, clinging to my mane, to Jasper's jeans, to Red's shirt. We were all coated with dirt and sweat and frustration. It had been a very long day and the sun wasn't even at its highest point in the sky.

I am five years old, Jasper is eleven, and Red is . . . tired. His hair has silvered like the muzzle of an aging stallion and the lines in his kind face are more deeply worn, as if he were a rock in a fast-running stream, grooved by the rushing water—or in Red's case, marked by the rush of time and care. *Careworn.* That is a lovely human word that Miz M uses about her husband.

Red might be tired, but right now he's intensely focused. On me. And I am not pleasing him. Jasper is sending out vibrations of anxiety, mirroring my own, though she is standing quietly, arms outstretched and palms down, pleading with me to understand, to cooperate.

I cannot, because I am afraid, and I am afraid of my very fear. Because this should be easy for me. I am an Arabian, I am the daughter of Sola, I am the second-ranked mare in the Cold Creek herd. I am Jasper's companion. It is my destiny to carry her, to achieve the partnership we have both longed for since we met two years before. I am smarter, faster, bolder, and more attuned to humans than most horses. And yet the pressure of Red's upper body leaning against my saddle has completely undone me.

"Let's take a break. Again." Red sighed and walked slowly over to the fence, favoring his left leg. Jasper joined him and they both drank deeply from bottles of water. I watched them, half wary, half ashamed, while kicking my heels in the corner of the corral, shaking off the saddle blanket and tossing my head in circles.

"You waited too long to start that filly," Bull complained in his high voice. "She's spoiled. Won't do nothin' but what she wants."

This was not the first time Bull, or Peach, had said

something like this, and Jasper, instead of flaring up as she usually did, hung her head. Red just frowned, his mouth disappearing into one sealed seam among the wrinkles of his face. I realized at that moment that he was even more stubborn than Jasper—that I probably wasn't going to win this battle of wills. I didn't really want to: I *wanted* to be led. And yet . . .

"Sami has more spirit than any horse I've ever seen," Red said, also not for the first time. "She's smart. She trusts us. It was right to start her slow. I don't want to touch that spirit."

"Well, right now you can't barely touch the horse, so I wouldn't worry." Peach grinned. He put an arm around Jasper's shoulder. "Cheer up, girl. Sami'll come around. Eventually."

.   .   .

I STOOD HOCK-DEEP IN THE STREAM, DREAM-ing over the familiar green tangle of trees, thinking about weight.

Weight means predators—a big cat sinking its claws on your back. Weight means pressure—a loss of momentum, stop-ping your flight. Weight is a burden—the end of childhood. Weight is an honor—carrying your companion.

I had come so far. My first lessons with bridling and

saddling were calm and easy. I had been ponied behind Chief, done weeks of groundwork under saddle and bridle. The guests at the ranch often watched my lessons, murmuring admiration of my gait, my flexion, my responsiveness. I had gained authority in the herd, until finally I was Magpie's undisputed second. *That will change if I can't bear a rider.*

I had reached a wall within myself, and I was frightened. Not of Red, not of Jasper. Of failing.

Surrounded though I was with friends, equine and human, with the luxurious beauty and space of the ranch, with food and drink and affection ... *why did I long for freedom? Freedom from leather and bit, girth and rope ... freedom from hands and human voices, from instruction and pressure. From weight. To be weightless.*

These feelings nipped and circled me like persistent horseflies, and I ran from them, as if I could put space between me and my tormentors. I plunged from the creek, through the woods, bursting onto the meadow with a whinny, and galloped until I had lost the last trace of the feel of weight on my back.

For a while, Buck ran with me, though he couldn't keep up for long. Of all the herd, the mustang understood my feelings the best. How he had reconciled them for himself, I did not know. I slowed my pace to allow him to run shoulder to shoulder with me, his long, coarse black-and-tan mane brushing against my neck. He must have run like this with his mares, when he was wild. How had he given up his freedom? Of all of us, only Buck had been born away from humans. And yet he was just as patient and obedient to Miz M as Magpie or Sunny. Even this gelding, who had known complete independence, who had been a wild, free animal, had learned what it seemed I could not: how to bear weight. I studied him as we slowed to a canter, then a jog. Buck bristled with controlled energy, head lifted to the wind in his constant lookout for threats and signals of change. Change. Buck had changed, certainly, but not his inmost nature. He had found a way to be a mustang and to be Miz M's horse. He seemed happy, and I most definitely was not.

If I was unhappy, I suspected that Jasper was even unhappier. I knew how much she wanted to sit on my back, to finally run with me, instead of trying to keep up by my side. But more than this, she was unhappy about the ranch. It was the end of summer and there had been only a few guests to fill the cabins and ride the horses. Cricket and Irish were out of condition, and even Dodger had put on a few pounds around his girth. Jasper rode all three of them, but they weren't the horses she wanted to be on. She wanted me, and I was failing her.

Buck suddenly threw up his head and came to a sharp stop. I overshot him, then cantered in a circle back to the place he held on the ridge, his right foreleg scraping the earth restlessly. It was obvious he had sensed something—but whether it was a real or imagined threat I did not know. *Something's coming,* he neighed. *Change.*

I hoped he meant me.

. . .

"PLEASE, DAD, *PLEASE* LET ME TRY!"

"I told you no, Jasper, and it's still no."

"But maybe you're too heavy for Sami! She's my horse—I should be the one who rides her first!"

"And your father has told you ad nauseum that an eleven-year-old girl has no business getting on an unbroke horse," Jasper's mother said.

"But what he's doing isn't working—everybody can see that! It's just the same over and over. . . ."

"Are you telling me you know more about starting a horse than your father does, young lady?"

"She's *my* horse, Mom!"

This, too, was a conversation I had heard before.

Jasper jumped up from her seat and ran into the house, leaving her parents alone on the twilit back porch facing the fields. In her absence, the conversation shifted.

"If things don't pick up, I'm afraid we're going to have to sell some of the horses, Gloria." Red's voice was somber.

"I know," Miz M replied softly. "But let's give it another year—another summer. We can afford that."

"Barely," Red grunted. "Probably if we put in some kind of spa, people would come. I don't know how many folks want to come and just ride and fish anymore. Seems like we're too rough around the edges for most."

"A spa . . ." Miz M's voice was amused. "Well, I could make mud wraps out of cow patties. Teach Bull how to do pedicures."

Red's laugh echoed across the field.

"Peach could be the yoga instructor," Miz M continued, "and you could . . . um, you could . . ."

"Move to another state."

Most of this was over my head, but their laughter— and there was a lot of it—comforted me, even as I fretted over Jasper's tears.

THE MOON WAS HIGH ABOVE THE FIR TREES and the herd had settled into the deep quiet of the darkest part of the night when a familiar sound broke through my dreams. At first I thought a wakeful robin was disturbing the peace, but then I pricked my ears and heard the whistle clearly: Dee *dee dee dee.* Jasper!

It had been a long time since she'd visited me this late, and curiosity put extra speed in my stride as I trotted toward the gate. I could just make out her small shadow perched on the fence, her hair swinging over her shoulders as she leaned toward me. Dee *dee dee dee,* she whistled again. And then I was by her side, our faces at the same height, and I took the carrot she held between her teeth, my muzzle grazing her cheeks. We both gazed out to the dark field, to the yellow moon furred in the humid, late-August sky.

"It's all right, Sami," Jasper said quietly, her small fingers tangling through my mane. I wasn't sure what exactly was all right, but I liked hearing her say it. Despite her words, I felt tension—excitement—in her body, her hands. Jasper often radiated this kind of energy, and I was accustomed to it.

"Let's get your bridle on," she suggested in the same

tone. And before I could wonder at her words, she slipped the leather straps over my ears and had the bit in my mouth. I didn't mind the bit, though Red wouldn't let me graze while wearing it. If Jasper wanted to go for a walk, I wished she'd chosen the halter. But Jasper showed no sign of leaving her perch on the fence, so I stood quietly, poking at the bit with my tongue and wondering what we were going to do next.

Jasper gave a gentle tug on the bridle and asked me to move nearer to the fence. I complied, and then I felt her hands across my back, stroking my withers, my barrel, my hindquarters. It was like a nice grooming without a currycomb, and I relaxed into it, leaving the bit alone and just enjoying Jasper's presence at this unusual time of night. The air was so soft it seemed to have lulled the woods and trees and everything in them to silence, to dreams. I was getting a bit dozy myself when I felt a very slight pressure on my back. I turned my head and saw that Jasper had placed one of her legs across the small of my back, as if I were a footrest. It wasn't very dignified, and Jasper didn't look all that comfortable, but if that's how she wanted to sit, it was fine with me. I sighed and resumed my contemplation of the night.

Jasper shifted her leg and put her hands on my mane—what was the girl up to?—and I put my weight on my left foreleg to keep my balance.

"It's okay, Sami, everything's okay," she said in the low, singsong voice she used when I was nervous. But I wasn't nervous now, though Jasper's legs seemed rather heavier and she was clutching my mane a little too tightly for comfort. I decided to walk up a step or two to ask her to lighten up her fingers. It worked—she released my mane and patted my neck. I felt a slight pressure on the bit and stopped.

"See, Sami," Jasper laughed shakily, "this isn't so bad." Her voice came from directly behind my head.

And that's when I realized—it wasn't Jasper's legs on my back. It was Jasper herself.

I froze. My body turned as rigid as the fence, except for my ears, which flickered back and forth in a frantic search for more information. I could hear Jasper taking deep breaths—it sounded like she was gulping the air. I swiveled my eyes back but I couldn't see all of her, just the points of her boots dangling at my sides. My mind raced as I tried to put together the pieces of feelings and instincts thrilling through me—*stay perfectly still . . . Run! . . . Wait and see what she does next. . . . Run! . . . She is so much lighter than Red. . . . Don't move a muscle. . . . If I move . . . if I move, what? She'll fall? I'll fall? Her weight will hinder my escape? And what am I escaping from? Certainly not from Jasper. She's . . . well, she's simply Jasper. I must not hurt her. She never, ever hurts me. Would she hurt me now? Would Jasper ever hurt me? Would she put me in danger? This weight . . . Run! Run! Can I run? This weight is Jasper. It's Jasper. Who would never hurt me. And I can run.*

I *had* to. I had to run to release my feelings, to test the weight, to see what I was when I was a horse under a rider. For just as humans are transformed by being astride a horse, we horses are transformed, too. We become, for our companions, more than horse, like Magpie and Sunny. Perhaps you think that horses were made to be ridden—that this sort of thing comes naturally to us. It should tell you something that even I, Samirah, Arabian mare bred to carry kings, had to dig deep for the courage to bear this strange—oh, strange, though so familiar!—weight.

So I ran. I could not contain myself—either the fear or the joy that propelled me forward in equal measure. I felt Jasper slip backward, her weight shifting toward my hindquarters, and I found myself naturally compensating with my stride, trying to keep us both balanced. The reins flapped against my neck, then tightened so I could feel a delicate tension communicating the words of Jasper's hands to my mouth. She had steadied herself, and she wasn't asking me to stop. I felt her legs grip my sides firmly, and after a few more strides, her seat settled down to join my back, moving with me. Moving with me! It was so strange, to have this small human, my own human, running along with me through the sweet, dense summer night! I always came to Jasper, followed Jasper, moved around Jasper—now she was moving with me! It was companionship. I finally understood it.

The shift from fear to wonder, wonder to joy, burst over me as if the sun had suddenly shot out from behind the fence of trees. I felt confidence rippling through my limbs, through the muscles of my body. I flared my nostrils to take in every particle of the soft, night-scented air, snorting loudly and throwing my tail high behind me, the streak of this new comet, new constellation, that was Jasper and Me. Jasper gave a gasping laugh as I bounded forward, delirious with my own speed, with the bewildering intoxication of running for the first time not alone, not side by side, but *with* another creature, as one. I knew at that moment that we would never part.

That I would never be alone. And that, for a horse, is the greatest thing of all.

"Okay, Sami, whoa, girl, whoa!" I felt pressure on my mouth, not sharp, but steady, and I reluctantly shortened my stride, then dropped to a trot, and finally to a walk, shaking my head and trembling a bit as I came down from the run. Jasper was laughing, a high, breathy, exultant sound, and she stroked my neck over and over again, praising me.

"I knew you were just waiting for me, Sami! You're the best, most beautiful, smartest, fastest . . ." Her words trailed into the night. I found myself relaxing by degrees, my breath evening, my mind and body settling. By the time we reached the gate, I was practically sauntering. Jasper held the reins loosely, and her legs swung free from my sides. We walked quietly, companionably, through the dark.

A flare of light and a bark of sound broke our reverie.

"Jasper Munk, what on God's great green earth do you think you're doing?!"

I threw my head sharply and stopped. There by the gate, illuminated by the glare of Red's big flashlight, stood Jasper's parents, fury flowing from their bodies and voices.

My instinct was to run, and so was Jasper's. I felt her body shift to the right, as if about to ask me to turn around, but then she stopped and recentered herself. I felt her stiffen her back and square her shoulders.

"I am riding my horse," she replied.

CHAPTER 5

Know ye there exists a mare

Swift

With highborne silken tail

———

IF I REMEMBER CORRECTLY, JASPER WAS PRAC-tically chained to the house for about a month, given the worst of the chores, lectured so often that I began to flee the sound of Red's cantankerous, self-righteous voice, and generally made to feel like a criminal.

But what her parents couldn't do was stop her from riding me. After all, as Jasper argued smugly, she had to continue my education or risk losing the gains she'd made.

And that made Red angriest of all. Or proudest, depending on how you looked at it.

For he could not deny that his daughter—his small, freckled daughter no bigger than a wildflower—had done what he could not. To Jasper and me, it was obvious. For Red, it was both maddening and miraculous. I had never smelled such fear as his and Miz M's when they discovered us that night, and it took some time for

that fear—and the anger it caused—to molt away and re-
veal pride.

So it was with mixed feelings that Red watched over
us, as anxious as a new broodmare, until eventually
even he could not deny that Jasper was safe with me.
That I had finally made the leap to be *more than horse* for
my companion.

More than horse? After a while, *she* became more
than rider. It seemed we could do anything. With Jasper's imagination and my natural abilities, the games of
the paddock took flight. Each month seemed to bring a
new story, a new trick or skill to learn. First she thought
she'd train us for the rodeo, and we spent hours racing
around makeshift barrels, chasing calves, herding the
other horses (I enjoyed that—especially when I got to
boss Magpie into a corner so Jasper could rope her).
Then Jasper wanted to try trick riding, and terrified her
parents by learning how to stand on my back at a canter, to leap aboard by jumping over my hindquarters,
to ride backward, sideways, and occasionally upside
down (though that was usually in error). She was utterly
fearless, and I made certain that she had every reason
to be.

But she still could sense when I was having an

untrained sort of a day, and those mornings we simply ran, as fast and as far as I desired.

Our range increased to the edges of the ranch and to the land that lay beyond it. Jasper, of course, was supposed to stay within its confines, which were large enough but not always large enough for us. I discovered that there were mountains beyond *our* mountains, the gentle curves that encircled the grassland, dusty brown and green with pines in summer, snow-tipped in winter, forming the comforting perimeter of our world. The *beyond* mountains were higher, harsher, thinner at top and rough sided. They plunged down to a mysterious landscape, far from our eyes, and a colder air seemed to blow from their direction. We followed the river, swam at the calm crossing where Jasper's ancestor had once sailed his ferry, and searched for the outlaws' cave. We kept riding the border of our known world, galloping its very rim.

. . .

IT WAS THE NEXT SPRING WHEN THEY STARTED taking the herd apart.

Irish—last, besides me, to arrive—was the first to leave. Buck had been wild all morning, galloping the fence line, then breaking back to corral the mares tightly together, jostling and bruising in his frantic attempts to keep us in one safe pack. I resisted to the best of my ability, the rest bore his mood in silence, and Magpie just stared at him. Finally, after receiving a painful nip near my tail, I bolted away as fast as I could, running for the nearby creek. I could hear Buck start after me, but with another spurt of speed, his hoofbeats were silenced. I waited awhile before venturing back, hoping his mustang mood had passed. By the time I rejoined the group at the fence, Irish was already in the trailer. The squeals coming from the barn told me that Buck had had to be confined to his stall.

I glanced questioningly at Magpie, then back to the trailer, where I could see Irish's head turned as far as possible toward us.

Leaving, Magpie told me. *This is good-bye.*

Good-bye, good-bye, good-bye . . . Our neighs sounded back and forth, down the fence, from the trailer, now churning up clouds of dust, and from the barn in Buck's desperately sad whinny. *Good-bye, good-bye.*

It is a difficult thing for a herd to lose a member. As horses, we are at once ourselves and parts making up a whole. The completeness and safety of our herd deeply affects us as individuals, just as the herd as a group is impacted by the health and disposition of each horse. We are, I suppose, like a human family, only more so.

I mourned the loss of Irish. I missed her calm presence, the sense of contentment and acceptance that you could not help but feel when you spent time with her. I hoped that the next place, her next herd, was kind to her. I wanted so much for her to have good fortune . . . perhaps because I suspected she hadn't in the past. That made me sorrowful—the idea that Irish might go to an unhappy place. It made the footing of our world seem slippery, uneven. And there were more good-byes to come. Eventually, even Buck grew accustomed to them.

Miz M, Bull, and Peach took the loss of the horses stoically, but Red and Jasper seemed to feel the succession of rattling trailers as body blows.

"It's not the end," Miz M would calmly remark, wiping her forehead with the back of her arm and gazing at Jasper with the clear, gray-blue eyes they shared. But Jasper's eyes were as dark as storm clouds, her lips pinched together in a line as thin as Red's. Father and daughter stalked the ranch with identical stiff, slow gaits, as if hunched under bad weather. But Miz M still whistled, Miz M still sang. I liked hearing her voice from the kitchen window as she baked bread and washed vegetables. She reminded me of Irish.

The worst day was when we lost both Julep and Bull.

"I can't pay you all that I owe you, but I can give you your horse," Red told Bull. Jasper didn't know what to cling to hardest—Bull's slim waist or Julep's brown neck. They didn't need a trailer—Bull packed the saddlebags, put on his hat, and mounted his horse.

"Now this should make you happy, Jasper," he said, trying to laugh. "Ain't this just like the old days? Cowboy riding off into the sunset?"

Jasper couldn't speak. She just stroked Julep's shoulder and held on to Bull's boot until they had to go, and we all stood and watched them trot down the drive and over the cattle guard and out onto the road. Then Jasper and her father walked like old men back into the house, and that day Miz M didn't sing.

. . .

BY AUTUMN, THE HERD HAD BEEN REDUCED TO Magpie, Chief, Buck, Sunny, and me. Even the Artful Dodger was gone, and in his case I was glad. We had all gotten an eyeful of the boy he now belonged to—small and sprightly as a water bug, with a whooping holler ten times his size—and he seemed like exactly the right companion for a pony like Dodger. I missed my friend, but I suspected he was happy.

We adjusted to the changes. At first the herd seemed like a ragged thing, with great holes where Julep, Cricket, Dodger, and Irish had been. (No one missed Zelda, who had been sold as a broodmare. Maybe a passel of foals was just what she needed, though I for one would not have wanted that mare for my dam.) But by the first snowfall, we had sorted ourselves out and were content again. Magpie was the uncontested leader, I was her second and Chief the third, and Sunny and Buck played their parts as grandfather and stallion. It was peaceful, having such an orderly and firm hierarchy. I was the only one who caused trouble.

Just as I had untrained days with Jasper, I had disobedient days with Magpie. I am the youngest of the herd, and I am proud. Sometimes I simply must break free from my bonds, show off my speed, my agility, ignoring Magpie's annoyance, stirring up Buck and even Chief to chase me over the fields. I feel such a mixture of things . . . both wanting to be a filly again, without rank or responsibility, and wanting to challenge Magpie, to be first in the herd. The combination makes me wild and restless, and unsuitable for company. It's an

odd coincidence that as Jasper reached her twelfth birthday she seemed to be feeling the same way. With the
loss of half the herd, and of Bull, she had aged, and the
burdens of the ranch hung heavily on her thin shoulders. She and Red would take me and Magpie out to
check for broken fence (an endless chore), and they
would discuss Cold Creek and its future. Mostly Red's
voice was casual, reassuring—*We've had to make changes,
but we'll see it through,* he'd say. Or: *You don't need to worry,
Jasper. Leave all that to your mother and me.* Or: *You've got
enough to think about with school and training Sami.* But I
could tell she didn't believe him. Didn't believe that he
wasn't worried, didn't believe that it wasn't her place
to help and to worry with him. I could feel tension in
every part of her body that touched me, and at times it
set me on edge.

But then there were mornings when Jasper came to
fetch me before sunrise and we struck off on a new trail,
abandoning the ranch and her chores for the entire day.
She'd be in trouble when we got back, but that's how
things are on an untrained day . . . a day when you need
to slip free from your bonds and be as irresponsible as a
foal. Our breath made clouds and we ran for warmth—I
am as surefooted in the snow as I would have been on

the sands where my ancestors raced, and Jasper as light and agile as any Bedouin boy. Two young girls who wanted trust and respect at the same time that they were running away from it. At least we had each other.

. . .

I DON'T KNOW WHAT I THOUGHT WAS HAPPEN-ing to Cold Creek, to us, the herd. I suppose I was too absorbed in my own changes, and in Jasper's, to wonder about what the future held for our families. There were fewer of us, horses and people, and more work. Spring was coming—you could just smell it buried deep in the snow, but rising. Life, grass, the hint of leaves on the buckthorn trees by the stream. Soon the first woodland stars peeped from clutches of rocks along the foothills of our mountains, and Jasper began gathering stalks of Blue-eyed Mary to weave in my tail braid. She had just started experimenting with different styles of braid, and I wished I could see them.

I knew that if we had no horses to ride—except for those belonging to the family—that must mean no guests were coming. As it turned out, a stranger did arrive, in May. He seemed very old to me, short and thin with a crooked sort of gait and white hair that tufted from his head like the filaments of a milkweed pod. He came one morning in a sky-blue pickup truck that groaned loudly down the drive, and moved into the smallest guest cottage, perched on a bluff overlooking our fields. I was surprised when he immediately sought out Sunny, bringing him carrots and a firm offer of friendship, which Sunny just as quickly accepted. Soon the two old-timers were making daily excursions around the property, never moving faster than a walk. The man rode with a sort of pack slung over his back, and he loaded Sunny's saddlebags with a variety of tools I didn't know the uses for.

Jasper seemed to understand them, and she was very curious about the old man, whom she called Mr. Sun. The day he arrived she kept her distance from him, mostly weeding the vegetable plot and playing tag with me. (Tag was a game I loved in which I would nip a soft cloth out of Jasper's hand and wave it around in my teeth until she managed to get it back from me. And then I'd steal it again. It was lovely.) The next day she was tied to the house, cooking and cleaning with Miz M, and only emerging at dusk to give me a tired hug and pat. But on the third day, when Mr. Sun had saddled Sunny, strapped on his pack, and they sauntered off toward the stream, Jasper quickly bridled me (she often rode me without a saddle) and we went off in pursuit.

We found them in one of our own favorite spots, where the brambly trees opened up into a small flowery meadow bound by the river and two tributaries, with a view of the *beyond* mountains in the distance. Sunny was untethered, cropping grass in the warm sunshine, and Mr. Sun was sitting on a rock, gazing at the mountains. If he heard our approach, he didn't indicate it. Jasper slid from my back and tied my reins in a knot, and I walked over to join Sunny while she cautiously approached the silent, still figure on the rock.

Sunny greeted me amiably, nibbling at my bridle, and I snuffled his mane. He was very clean—Mr. Sun groomed him well.

My companion, Sunny said.

I didn't know what he meant at first. Sunny didn't have a companion, really, though he was treasured by both the human family and the herd. He had been around for so long . . . been calm and loving and accepting of so many riders, of so many new horses. . . . I didn't really think of him as needing, or wanting, his own person. He belonged to all of us.

Mr. Sun. Sunny. We have the same name. I think I've been waiting for him.

I stared at the old palomino, swaybacked and

gray-whiskered but strong. His expression was gentle, as usual, but there was a new, soft spark in his eyes.

It is good he is light. We are old. We can be old together. We will take walks and stand in the sunshine. The spark flared up as Sunny gazed at the man, then he lowered his head to graze again.

I'm glad, I managed to say, but I was unsettled. Sunny had a companion—now all of us did—but surely Mr. Sun would be leaving. And the thought of the old gelding's sorrow made my heart beat too hard. Sunny . . . our grandfather, our rock . . . suddenly vulnerable because of this small old human. It was all very strange.

Meanwhile, Jasper and Mr. Sun were having their own conversation. He was showing her his tools, which looked to me like a stiff sheet lying on a board, a black stick, and a very small brush. He moved his hands over the sheet with the brush and Jasper watched him intently. I couldn't figure out what he was doing, so I resumed grazing until Jasper called me over to introduce me to Mr. Sun.

"Ah, an Arabian!" His features seemed to disappear into a maze of lightly scored lines as he smiled. "My daughter has an Arabian. A gray stallion named Shan, which means 'lightning' in Chinese."

My ears pricked. *Shan.* It was a noble name, like Samirah.

Jasper was similarly impressed. "Shan," she whispered. "That's beautiful." She paused. "So, do you, like, speak Chinese mostly?"

"Good lord, no!" Mr. Sun laughed. "I know a little, mostly words for food, but Emily, my daughter, studied it in school. She's probably the first person in the family since my grandfather to speak it fluently."

"Was it your grandfather who emigrated?" Jasper asked. I could tell she was feeling a little shy, but I don't know if Mr. Sun noticed. Jasper could be funny that way, skittish around people though so bold about most everything else.

"No, my great-grandfather. In fact, he was one of the workers who built the last ten miles of track that connected the transcontinental railroad, over in Promontory. That was back–"

"In 1869," Jasper interrupted. "Wow! That's like . . . *legendary!*"

"You know your history, young lady." Mr. Sun nodded.

"I love the old Western stuff." Jasper shrugged, but she was pleased. "Our ranch was started in the 1880s."

"Beat you here." Mr. Sun winked at her and she laughed.

I heaved a sigh to signal to Jasper that I wanted to return to Sunny, and she let me go. My girl and Sunny's old man spent an hour together, talking and looking at Mr. Sun's hands as he worked with his odd tools. As I watched how companionable they seemed, I had a feeling Sunny and I were going to be spending a lot more time together. I was both wrong and right, as a change came that even Buck couldn't have foreseen.

CHAPTER 6

To whom is it that I am going to yield thee up? . . .
Return with me, my beauty! my jewel!
And rejoice the hearts
of my children!

———

IT HAPPENED SO SUDDENLY, LIKE A SUMMER
lightning strike.

Except no, there had been storm clouds gathering for
a long time . . . the dispersal of the herd, Bull's leaving . . .
Red's ever-present, physically palpable stress. And I get
mixed up in my memories, for part of that summer *was*
peaceful, after the arrival of Mr. Sun. For a month,
maybe more. Then the old man told Jasper that when
he left Cold Creek, he'd be taking Sunny with him.

"Dad's selling him to you?" Jasper was shocked, but
I was glad. It would have broken Sunny's heart to be left
behind.

Mr. Sun nodded. "He'll go with me to my daughter's. You know, my wife died this year, so I'm going to
live with Emily's family. This summer . . . was my time
to say good-bye to Mrs. Sun, to say good-bye to my old

life. I needed solitude for painting and thinking, but I also got two very good friends." First he patted Sunny, then Jasper.

"Okay," was all that Jasper whispered.

"I'm glad you approve. I hope you find good homes for the rest of the horses, especially Sami."

I think Jasper and I flinched at the same time.

"What?" We both stared at him. Mr. Sun suddenly looked alarmed and reached for Jasper's hand.

"Your father told me he was thinking seriously of selling the ranch. Did I misunderstand?" His voice was soft but I could feel the tension in it.

Jasper was silent for a long time, her posture frozen. Then she slowly untangled herself from her seated position and rose stiffly. She walked to my side, pulled herself into the saddle, but did not ask me to move forward. She seemed to have frozen again.

"Jasper?" Mr. Sun said again. "I may have been mistaken. Please forgive me if I've upset you."

Still, my companion seemed stuck, unable to speak or move.

"I should not have said anything, Jasper." Now Mr. Sun sounded very worried. "You should speak to your mother and father directly. I hate to think that I've caused you pain, when surely—"

"You're probably the only one who bothered to tell me the truth." Jasper's voice was broken with tears.

Suddenly her heels dug urgently into my sides, but I needed no encouragement. I wheeled around and we ran as fast as I could carry us back to the ranch. Jasper's breath came in sobs and I felt a wild energy coursing through her, and through me. I had to find Magpie. Surely Magpie would know what was happening. I plunged through the creek, scrambled up the bank, and pounded through the meadow, my breath sounding close to sobs, too.

I was dismayed when Jasper led me to the barn instead of putting me out in the field. Her hands were trembling as she hastily untacked me and slid the stall door shut behind her. I neighed at the top of my lungs to her, to Magpie, to Buck and Chief, rushing toward the door, then swinging my hindquarters around in a frantic circle as I paced my confines. Finally I heard Magpie's answering whinny:

"What's wrong? What is it?"

Then Buck: "Forest fire! Is there a forest fire?" (Of course he would go straight to something like that.)

Chief simply neighed: "Sami girl? Hold on there, filly. I'm on my way."

Sure enough, I soon heard the steady *clop-clop* of

Chief's hooves across the driveway, and I smelled Peach's signature cattle-and-coffee scent.

"Jasper?" Peach called out as she pelted into the house. "Where's the fire?"

I hoped that wouldn't start Buck off again, but I wasn't sure how much he actually understood of human speech, anyway.

Peach put Chief in the cross-ties at the front of the barn and went to get the clippers (Chief for some reason was quite furry and needed his bridle path and hocks clipped fairly frequently when it was hot). I could just see my friend from between the bars of my stall door and trumpeted to him again.

"The herd! Leaving! Jasper's upset! I'm upset!"

"Magpie didn't say so," Chief snorted. "All's well, filly. Calm down. Buck ain't sensed it."

"Mr. Sun is taking Sunny!"

That gave Chief pause. He looked at me for a long time.

"We'll miss him," he sighed.

Chief didn't understand. Magpie and Buck didn't understand. They didn't hear what Mr. Sun had said.

"We're losing our home!" I whinnied.

"I just don't think so, Sami," Chief whickered. "Everything's going to be all right."

That was always Chief's attitude. I usually found it comforting, but right now it was infuriating. But there was nothing I could do: I was stuck in my stall and had to wait. I paced in circles while Chief was clipped, banged my hooves against the door when he was led out, causing Peach to actually holler at me, and went around and around in frustration as the sun set and the ranch quieted. I longed to be in the pasture . . . I longed for Magpie, my leader . . . but mostly I longed for Jasper. Whatever was happening, we needed to face it together.

· : ·

I MUST HAVE FALLEN ASLEEP AT SOME POINT during that long night, for I was woken by Jasper quietly slipping into my stall and whispering *shhhhhh*. She was carrying my saddle and bridle, plus an old set of saddlebags that I'd worn before on our longer rides. Everything smelled as if it had been recently oiled, and one saddlebag was already packed, for it was heavier than the other. Jasper slipped me a carrot from her pocket and quickly finished tacking me up. Her hands were no longer trembling—she moved swiftly, I would say, almost furiously. I stood very still, at attention, letting her work without interference. She picked my hooves, then put the pick in the empty saddlebag, along with my currycomb, brush, and several additional items from the tack room. Then she strapped a roll of blankets behind the saddle's cantle and wedged another roll of material in front, under the horn.

"Sami, I hope this is comfortable," she said in a low voice. It was—unfamiliar, but not irritating. I stood calmly to let her know I was fine. "Good girl," Jasper said, and patted my shoulder. As she led me from the stall, I realized that all the things on my back *were* fairly heavy, and would be more so once Jasper was aboard. I watched her pull her arms through the straps of her own pack, and then she gingerly mounted me, taking care to settle lightly on the saddle. Definitely heavier than I was used to, but I could carry this weight and more if Jasper needed. I may only be a shade over fourteen hands, but that has always been more than enough for an Arabian, even cavalry mounts like several of my great-great-aunts and -uncles.

I don't think it was until we stepped from the barn out onto the driveway that I really considered what we were doing. I had been so absorbed in Jasper's preparations and in doing my best to be cooperative that I hadn't thought through what they meant. We walked slowly out into the darkest part of the night, when the crickets have quieted and the land seems very lonely and strange. This is the time of night when the herd always gathers closest, forming a protective circle against the dark and all that the dark holds. But Jasper and I were not seeking protection. Nor was this the beginning of a lighthearted, untrained day—that I knew from my companion's fierce concentration as well as by the hour of night.

Jasper and I were running away.

We didn't go through the gate into the pasture, where most of our adventures started. Instead Jasper guided me to the strip of grass between the driveway and the fence line and we headed toward the entrance to the ranch, which was protected by the cattle guard but had no gate. As I walked quietly along the fence, I could hear the herd stirring nearby, alerted, no doubt, by Buck that something unusual was happening. We were about halfway down the drive when Magpie's figure broke away from the dark night and became visible.

"It's okay, Mags," Jasper whispered. Magpie raised her head and nickered an inquiry to me.

"*Shhhhh,* Magpie!" Jasper hissed.

I understood what Jasper wanted—it was like playing Indian scout. I paused by the fence and my chestnut muzzle reached for Magpie's white one.

"Good-bye," I breathed.

"Not for long, though. Take care of your girl."

"I will."

I don't know why or how Magpie believed that this wasn't a permanent good-bye—like Irish's, like Dodger's . . . like Sunny's would be. But her confidence comforted me as I picked my way along the grass as noiselessly as possible. We crossed the cattle guard, and Jasper stopped me to look back at the ranch. All was dark and silent, except for the first trills of the mountain bluebirds, which meant that dawn was on its way. And with a last farewell glance at the sleeping house and fields, so were we.

. . .

THE SUN WAS WELL UP WHEN WE REACHED THE outlaws' cave—a narrow gash in the rocky mountainside that was quite hard to spot unless you knew where to look. We had picnicked at this spot many times before, and after taking a long drink from the stream, I settled down to graze. Jasper rummaged through her pack and pulled out some of her own food, but it remained in her hand, uneaten, as she lay back against a rock and stared straight ahead with reddened eyes.

We had a beautiful, long view of the land from

here, and Jasper and I gazed out at the wildflower-filled foothills all morning, absorbing the quiet, drinking the stream's cold water and the mountainside's clean air. After I was thoroughly watered and rested, I felt suddenly, well, *playful.* I knew Jasper's spirits were very low, and I knew I should be feeling serious. I had been saddled with a great responsibility, and I had probably just lost my herd and my home. Nevertheless, my blood was singing, and I was full to the brim with lively animal spirits. We were on an adventure! I wanted a flower or two in my forelock, perhaps some paint around one eye. Or maybe we could just play tag.

I looked over at Jasper. She was still sitting in the shade, her knees pulled in and her arms wrapped tightly around them. She looked like a turtle trying to get all its limbs tucked inside its shell. Her face was hidden in the crook of her elbow, and her fingers curled around a red bandanna that she'd been using to wipe her face. Casually, as if I were strolling over to a new patch of grass, I made my way up the slope. I was quite good at moving quietly, and Jasper didn't stir, even when I was nearly at her side. I stretched out my neck, leaned forward as far as I could without taking another step, and lipped the bandanna free.

Jasper's head shot up, her mouth a little circle of surprise. I crab-stepped back and shook the cloth in my teeth. The expression on her wet face softened. I nodded my head up and down, then gave another big shake as I pawed at the gravelly rocks that littered the slope. Jasper smiled. Finally I sauntered back toward her, as if I didn't care whether or not she got the bandanna back from me. Just as she reached out her hand to take it, I whirled away, cantering down the slope and throwing my head around like a dog with a rabbit. Jasper sprang to her feet with a laughing shout and flew after me, calling, "Okay, Sami, you win!"

We chased each other over the grassy slope, through the creek, in circles and arabesques and pirouettes. (Well, I pirouetted at least. Jasper was a bit clumsier in her boots.) Eventually I let her steal the cloth back, and then she tied it around her head and jumped on my back, which was clever. She leaned back to rest her head on my hindquarters, and sighed.

"Oh, Sami, what are we going to do? I mean, Mom's probably flipping."

Well, I'd sort of gotten used to the idea of running away, but I did not want to upset Miz M, either.

"I just wish they could say for *certain* one way or the

other. It's always *maybe* we'll have to . . . *We'll just have to see*. . . .

"Dad *says* he'd never sell you, but what are we going to do if we lose the ranch?"

I breathed a deep sigh of relief, and Jasper laughed.

"Sometimes I think you really understand what I'm saying, Sami."

Of course I did. It was humans who had difficulty with communication. I'm an Arabian. I understand more than most. Now I understood that Jasper was torn: torn between her love for her family and her love for me. We had to be together—that was obvious—and her family had to understand that. What if we went back . . . and Red went back on his word?

Just then a light breeze picked up, eddying between the mountainside and the stream. I raised my head automatically to taste the air and to read whatever it had to say. I pricked my ears sharply: The breeze carried the scent of another horse. I breathed in again. Sunny! My welcoming neigh was so loud that I startled Jasper off my back. *Oh dear, I hope we weren't still being quiet.*

Jasper dusted her legs and seat and raised her hand to her eyes, squinting into the bright sunshine.

"What, Sami? What is it?" She sounded a little

nervous, so I stood calmly to let her know that there was nothing to fear. Still, she hastily bridled me and remounted. By that time I could hear Sunny making his way around the side of the hill that hid the outlaws' cave. He was carrying someone—no doubt Mr. Sun. I neighed again and heard Sunny's answering whinny. A few moments later, Jasper called out, "Mr. Sun?" and he waved to her, moving Sunny into a slow jog that was the fastest I'd ever seen the two old-timers go.

"I thought you might be here." Mr. Sun sounded winded. He smiled faintly as he caught his breath.

Jasper didn't reply, but sat very stiffly on my back.

I greeted Sunny, who seemed in fine spirits, pleased to be out with his companion, and to see me. This was a place we'd visited often with our humans.

"Everyone's all right?" I asked him.

"Seems so. Except for the people. Red and Miz M are having fits. And Buck. He's having fits about the weather."

I looked about me at the cloudless blue sky and felt the freshening breeze. It was very hot and dry, but we were in the height of summer. At least the wind was lively.

"I brought you some lunch," Mr. Sun said. He swung

his leg over Sunny's back and carefully lowered himself to the ground. He took a few things out of the saddlebags, then tied Sunny's reins and let him loose.

I joined Sunny as he eased down to the stream to drink, and we stood and swished flies together while Jasper and Mr. Sun talked and ate. It didn't seem like he was cheering her up. I had done a much better job with tag. Her voice and her body sagged, and I felt my own uneasiness return.

"I don't know," Jasper was saying. "I guess I felt—it's just so awful thinking about losing Cold Creek. I know running away doesn't make a lot of sense. But I've got to keep Sami, no matter what happens." Her voice trailed off again.

Our companions ate in silence for a while. Then Jasper said, "They don't tell me anything. It's like I'm not really a part of things. I mean, do they think they can just sell the ranch without me noticing?" She gave a laugh that didn't really sound like one.

Mr. Sun made a noise between a grunt and a sigh.

"They want to protect you," he told her.

"By keeping things from me—by *lying* to me?" Her voice was outraged.

"I don't think your father lied to you, Jasper,"

Mr. Sun said mildly. "And I don't think he'll break his promise about Sami."

"If he does, I'll run away for good," Jasper promised haughtily.

"So this isn't 'for good'?" Mr. Sun asked.

Jasper was quiet for a while. Sunny stamped a hoof to shake off flies. I raised my muzzle to the gusty breeze, wondering why Buck was worried about the weather. The air smelled dry, saturated with late-summer heat, dry pine needles, dust from the bare patches of earth on the mountainside.

"I'm going to stay here for a while," Jasper finally said. "Would you tell Mom and Dad? That I'm okay and all? I just want to be alone—well, with Sami."

"You're never really alone as long as you have her. Is that how you feel?" Mr. Sun's voice was warm with affection and understanding.

"That's just how I feel," Jasper said, and she started to cry again. Mr. Sun put his arm around her and she hid her face in his shoulder.

"How long is 'awhile,' Jasper?" he asked her gently. "Your parents are very worried, you know."

I couldn't hear her answer, muffled against Mr. Sun's arm, but it seemed to satisfy him.

"Let's take a look at your supplies and make sure you have everything you need." Jasper hugged him, took the bandanna off her head and blew her nose into it, and the two of them put away the lunch things and began to rummage through my saddlebags.

I like campouts, Sunny commented. *You get marshmallows and new flavors of grass. Your humans sleep near you. When I live with Mr. Sun we will camp out.*

Personally, I thought Mr. Sun seemed too old for such doings, but I refrained from mentioning it.

"Well," Sunny's companion said, "you've got more food for Sami than you do for yourself. And you forgot a can opener for the beans. You got a pocketknife?" Jasper shook her head, and Mr. Sun reached into his jeans and handed her one.

"You're going to have to eat your dinner cold. Don't start a fire in this weather. You should be warm enough with your sleeping bag in that cave. Now let's see about where Sami can spend the night."

I watched Jasper and Mr. Sun make their way around what was now our campsite, inspecting trees and boulders. Finally, the old man helped Jasper rig up a picket line between two medium-sized pine trees. They spent a while fussing with the ropes until Mr. Sun seemed satisfied. It was getting on to late afternoon when he mounted Sunny and we said our good-byes.

"Jasper, I can't promise that your folks won't come tearing out here to fetch you, but I'll try to hold them off."

"Thanks, Mr. Sun. Thanks for everything." Jasper's voice was stronger now, clearer.

"Well, I ran away myself once when I was about your age. Except I only got about a half mile away when I realized I forgot my paintbrushes, and there didn't seem much use in leaving home without them. I was back in time for dinner. I think you're going to have a better adventure than I did."

They laughed, and Sunny and I whickered to each other. Jasper and I watched the old man and the elderly gelding amble away until their figures disappeared into the glare of the strong summer sun. Jasper gave me a brisk pat.

"Come on, Red Bandit," she said, grinning. "Let's go be outlaws."

CHAPTER 7

Alert

She leaps from danger's path.
Her round jet-hued hooves
Ravish the earth

————

THAT DAY–THE REMAINS OF IT–WAS ONE OF the happiest Jasper and I had ever spent together.

We cantered down the stream, my hooves sending sprays of water that made Jasper shout with laughter and cooled my flanks and chest. The stream was filled with flickering fish that scattered at our approach, slivers of rainbowed silver within the silver water. We circled the base of the mountain that hid the outlaws' cave, and Jasper picked wildflowers for my forelock and tail, just as I'd wished. We stood in flower-dazzled meadows and watched the blue begin to dim from the sky. We listened to the evening song of bluebirds and buntings, and heard the whistles of osprey hunting fish. We were no longer the kept creatures of Cold Creek Ranch–there to work and to serve–we were wild creatures of the West itself!

Of course we both loved Cold Creek, and I couldn't imagine another home. But still—this freedom was intoxicating. I pictured days of nomadic wandering, just Jasper and me, perhaps to the *beyond* mountains . . . and beyond them. Arabians were meant for this sort of life. As I said, we carry our home with us, in our very blood. As Jasper and I watched the dark shapes of birds skylark across the crimsoning clouds, I felt as if this hour was a summation of us: horse and girl, free but encircled in our bond. Companions.

It was growing dark by the time we made our way back to the campsite. The sky had clouded, and the night was coming on quickly. I wasn't very sweaty, especially since Jasper was riding bareback, but she still gave me a nice sponging off with water from the stream, then filled a travel water bucket and hauled it over to the picket line that she and Mr. Sun had strung. She fixed a long lead rope to the picket line, testing it with the weight of her body, then, satisfied that it would hold, she clipped the other end to my halter. There was no need for this, I felt. I was far too smart to wander off and get lost in the night. Besides, I would never leave Jasper alone out here. I lowered my neck and found that I could easily reach the water bucket, some grass, and had room to lie down if I wanted. Jasper then brought over a measure of oats in the improvised bucket of her cowboy hat. My muzzle is small, so I had no trouble eating from it. First she held the hat for me, stroking my neck and shoulder, then, as I got a little more energetic with my food, she put the hat next to the water bucket and went to fix her own dinner.

We ate together in the gathering darkness. There were no stars, no moon visible above. Jasper sang a little, and I finished my oats.

"You know, Sami, I think I'd rather sleep out here with you than in that cave. I mean—bats." She sounded a little nervous.

I was glad. I wanted her company, too. My ancestors slept in the same tent as their Bedouin families, and that was something Jasper and I hadn't shared before.

She fetched a flashlight from the saddlebags and spent some time tidying up the camp, then unrolled her sleeping bag under a pine tree a few yards away from me, clearing rocks from the ground and piling up pine needles. Then she came over to my picket line and did the same for my area, which was very thoughtful. She crawled into the sleeping bag, switched off the flashlight, and we looked out into the darkness together. It was very, very dark and the air was growing cooler. The breeze that had followed us all day was still around, ruffling the trees and making lonely noises from the mouth of the cave. I imagined the sands of the great desert, and the little oasis that a family made amid its vastness. We had our own protective circle here, in this American West, in the shadow of the mountain. The circle was *horse and child and horse and child....* What other creatures can take care of each other so well? The circle was our campsite, our home under the hidden stars. The circle was Sami and Jasper.

It took a long time for Jasper to fall asleep, but when she did, I finally did, too.

. . .

WIND. A STRANGE WIND. LIGHTS. STRANGE LIGHTS. I woke up with a shudder, my flanks quivering, my head thrown back violently. *Weather. Buck.* I might not have his extraordinary instincts, but my senses screamed, *Alarm, alarm!* I could make out Jasper's sleeping form, curled up in a little ball in her bag. She looked very small, like a foal sleeping under her mother's legs. I stood stock-still, ears, eyes, and nostrils straining to gather information. This was not the playful breeze of the day, and the lights were not the sun, nor the moon and stars. And I knew I had to wake her. I had to warn her. I let out a trumpeting blast: *Jasper! Storm! Storm!*

Just at that moment, the thunder exploded.

I have never heard anything like it. The deafening *crack* seemed like it would break my body in two. I reared to my height, maddened by the noise. When I plunged to earth, my forelegs became tangled up in something, and the sensation of restraint, of anything preventing my flight, made me sick with terror. I reared again, screaming.

A blinding light accompanied the horrific noise, and suddenly I could not see. It was like the world was ending. I plunged forward in a frenzy, only to smack my muzzle against a rope. I threw myself backward, pulling as hard as I could against the restraint. I tossed my head furiously, forelegs pawing at the sky, down and up, down and up, until I heard a frantic voice calling my name, heard the pounding of boots, and felt hands reaching for my muzzle, grasping at the halter.

I quite literally couldn't think. The noise had compressed all thoughts into one overwhelming imperative: *Run.* I was so consumed that the rest of the world seemed very far away . . . and it took a long, dangerous moment before Jasper could reach me, could get inside my fear to remind me of myself, of her. That there was a world outside that catastrophic sound. Finally, as the sky rumbled and the eerie lights continued to flicker in the low bellies of the clouds, something of Jasper's smell penetrated my brain, and I felt her trembling hands on my muzzle, heard her *shhhhhhhh, easy, easy, easy, Sami . . .* and reason returned. Not a lot, I'm afraid: I was still petrified. But I wasn't about to try to gallop off a cliff anymore.

I stood shaking like the needles of the pine trees around our campsite while Jasper tried to pack, dropping things, cursing, then finally crying out:

"What am I doing? I've got to get us away from the trees, Sami!"

She was right. I now understood clearly that we were in some sort of strange storm—all wind and cloud and flickering fire with no rain—and needed shelter. Jasper shoved a few things in her backpack, threw it over her shoulders, and ran back to me. She put my bridle on over my halter and unclipped me from the picket line. For a moment she stood rooted by my shoulder, surveying the land around us, trying to decide what to do. The landscape came in and out of view as the bluish light danced in the clouds above.

"The cave," she said. "C'mon, Sami, let's go!"

I bounded forward, and she staggered to keep up, tripping over my saddle, which lay on the ground by the sleeping bag, her boots dragging as I pulled her ahead. I was desperate to get us both to a protected place. But when we reached the mouth of the cave, a narrow defile carved in rock, it took a great deal of convincing on Jasper's part to get me inside. The air was stale and close and smelled of bats and the droppings of other animals, possibly big cats. I was stuck between the freakish weather and the dark, enclosed space: Not a choice any horse wants to make. But Jasper finally persuaded me to take a few steps, then another few, then another, until we had made it through the entrance and were inside.

The cave was extraordinarily dark. Even after my eyes adjusted, I still could only perceive a very rough outline of the cavern. It was small and relatively shallow, but I could feel space above my head and sensed movement within that space: bats. As long as they didn't fly into me, I wasn't bothered by their presence. I smelled mammal droppings, but they were old, so Jasper, I, and the bats were probably the only current guests here. I turned around to face the entrance and found that I could only see the outside world indirectly. We had entered the cave at an angle, then had to step around a large boulder that formed a corner, so you couldn't quite see the mouth itself from the body of the cave, which made it an excellent hiding place indeed. So I watched the flickering lights illuminate the boulder and flinched every time the thunder growled in the wild night outside. There were more lightning strikes, but the sound was muffled by the rocks of the mountain that enclosed us. We were birds, chased to earth by a storm.

We didn't have much room to move around, so Jasper hoisted herself up onto a ledge of rock and sat cross-legged, leaning against her backpack, one hand on my lead rope. I was still trembling a little, strung up to my highest pitch every time a *crack* sounded outside. I kept waiting for the rain to start, but it never did. Eventually, I felt the rope slacken and knew that Jasper was dozing on her roost. I also felt an unexpected whisper of calm, and I relaxed a fraction. We had done well, I thought. We were together. We were safe. Jasper had made the right decisions and I had trusted her. I flicked my tail and snorted and would have liked a carrot. I hoped that one was among the items Jasper had managed to pack up.

. . .

I THOUGHT THAT THE STORM WAS MOVING OFF.
Its noise was fading, and the hair-tingling scent of lightning had lessened. But the wind still gusted past the
cave's mouth, sending eddies of strangely hot air about
my knees and hocks. And then the wind brought a new
smell—only traces of it at first—a harsh odor that irri-
tated the lining of my nostrils. I snorted, then breathed
in again. The smell was stronger. *Smoke.*

The wind swept in another direction and the scent
was gone. But I was positive I had smelled it, and knew
what it was—the same smell as the piles of leaves that
Peach burned in late autumn, the smell that came from
the chimneys of the ranch. Smoke. *Fire.*

Just then Jasper awoke, and I heard her yawn and
shift position, stretching her legs. I stamped my hoof
and gave a low whinny.

"It's okay, Sami," she said. "Sounds like the storm's
almost gone. I'm going to go look around." I nickered
anxiously to her, but she just patted my side and handed
me a carrot from her backpack.

"Be right back." My companion felt her way along
the rock until she reached the boulder, then followed it
to the mouth of the cave, slipping out of my view. But
not for long: I was right behind her.

I peered over Jasper's shoulder, and she automatically put her arm under my neck, her hand reaching up to stroke my cheek. We looked out into the wild night.

Above us, the sky was as black as a bird's wing, and as full of flight, wind whipping the storm clouds forward. What visibility we had came from the east, where streaks of lightning pulsed the sky, illuminating the landscape in sudden bursts and casting eerie shadows. Then the wind changed direction again, and I saw another source of light, a sort of glow coming down the side of the mountain, toward the path that Sunny and Mr. Sun had taken this morning. If it hadn't been the wrong time, I might have thought the sun was rising. But with the glow came the acrid smell again: *Smoke*.

"Smoke," Jasper whispered. "Oh no, Sami."

A second later, a wall of flame rose from the mountainside.

It happened so impossibly fast, neither of us had time to think. I immediately started forward, and in another instant Jasper was on my back. I bolted away from the flames, away from the smoke that threatened to engulf us. I felt Jasper slip off center, grab at my mane, then plant her knees firmly to my sides. Instinctively, I plunged down to the base of the mountain, toward the stream. I could just make out our former campsite; the pine trees that held my picket line were twin torches burning from roots to tip. I swerved hard, then stopped abruptly, spinning on my hind legs. The mountain was on fire. The east was on fire. North, toward home, was so choked with smoke that I couldn't tell what lay ahead. I let out one panicked whinny, then threw myself and Jasper westward.

It was a nightmarish ride through a world of nightmare. Blazing tree limbs tumbled down the mountain, and the grass and flowers of the meadow were scorched black with flame. Soon my nostrils, throat, and lungs were aching terribly. The air itself was almost too hot to breathe. I ran blindly, away from the fire that screamed like a great cat in pursuit. The sound filled my ears as the smoke and heat choked my nostrils and burned my eyes. Jasper's face was buried in my mane, her arms clutched around my neck. Together we ran through the inferno.

Worse than the fire was the smoke. Worse than the smoke was the wind. For the wind controlled everything— where the smoke and fire went, where we went. I ran toward the cleanest air—but when the wind shifted, we were buffeted in a searing current, enveloped in thick, choking clouds. And then it would change course again, and I could breathe freely and see clearly, at least for a moment. I ran my fastest then, scarcely aware of the ground beneath me, my muscles straining to propel us forward and away.

I don't know how long I ran from the smoke. I don't know how long it took for the first rays of morning to penetrate the orange clouds rising from the mountain we had left behind. But eventually the air was clean enough for me to register other things: the emergence of an unfamiliar landscape, the feel of rock and slope under my hooves. I was exhausted, my body drenched with sweat, my limbs throbbing painfully. On my back, Jasper seemed stuck to me like a burr: She had hardly changed position since our flight began.

I was just beginning to slow my pace, to try to get my bearings, when it happened. The ground disappeared under my front hooves, and for a terrible moment my forelegs scrabbled in space. Then I was falling, and Jasper was falling with me.

My hooves hit dirt, not rock, and to stop my momentum I tried to collapse my body backward, to fold up my hind legs and skid, anything to not flip over my forelegs and somersault. I managed it—barely—but it was not enough to save Jasper. I felt her weight leave my back as her body tumbled headfirst over my neck and into the canyon below.

. . .

I LAY ON MY BELLY, TREMBLING, WAITING FOR more light. I needed every sense at its keenest to determine what to do. And I wasn't sure if I could stand up yet.

It seemed a long time before full dawn, the sun's rays obscured by the smoke billowing in the east. It was a murky sunrise, but the sky directly above was clear and clean; in fact, the fire seemed very far away from this strange red valley. I could see rock outcrops all around me, interspersed with gravelly, dry soil forming trails downward. I stretched out my forelegs, testing the loose dirt about me. I had landed on a sort of ledge, not very large, but large enough to have given me room to stop myself. Slowly, and with a groan, I rose up on weak legs and gave my body a shake. Everything hurt: my chest, my throat, my nostrils, my legs, my shoulders. But I could stand up and I could walk. I took a tentative step forward and peered over the lip of the ledge that held me.

The valley was a breathtaking sight. Red rock, green brush, brown earth spilled down to a sandbar, dotted with grasses, which abutted a wide, flowing, clear river. On its far side, red cliffs rose dramatically skyward, and I dared not think what our fate would have been had we fallen *there*. But this side of the river had a gentler incline, and it was obviously used as a water trail for many animals. I smelled goats and elk, and older hints of cattle and horses. This was a place Jasper and I would have loved to discover together, under different circumstances. I couldn't be sure, but I thought we were somewhere in the embrace of the *beyond* mountains.

I started down the trail, picking my way forward with great care. With every step, I peered around me and sniffed the air for Jasper. My nostrils still burned, but not as badly, and my eyes had stopped watering. I wanted very much to get to the river and to drink, but I wanted even more to find my companion. Where was she? Why hadn't she come back for me? I was used to Jasper falling off, and she always got right back on. Had she lost her way?

And then I heard a noise, the low moan of an animal in pain. It seemed to come from several yards to the right of the trail, and below, on the far side of a group of rocks. I decided to go farther along the trail, then double back. It would be easier to see what it was from below.

First I saw a boot, then a bare foot. A leg in a tattered pair of jeans. Movement: a hand clawing at rock. A flash of red hair: Jasper!

I bounded stiffly toward her and she let out a glad, hoarse cry. She reached toward me, then cried out again, in pain.

I had found Jasper. But Jasper couldn't move.

CHAPTER 8

The day we pushed on our steeds homeward the way
they had gone,
with hoofs chipped, jaded and worn by onset again and again;
And the galloping steeds came home with streaks of blood on
their breasts. . . .

———

"OH, SAMI! YOU'RE ALL RIGHT! YOU'RE ALL right!" Tears streamed down Jasper's sooty face, leaving blurred trails. My heart bounded up at the sound of her voice, and my eyes drank her in. My companion. We were together again.

"Sami, I need water. And we've got to go home. What if the fire—what if Cold Creek . . ." She started coughing and half-crying again. Then she spit onto the rocks, cleared her throat, spit again, and wiped her face off with her shirt.

"I think I hit my head pretty hard," she said. Her voice was raspy, harsher than normal. "I don't remember what happened after I fell. But my arm doesn't seem to be working all that great." She tried to raise her left arm and grimaced.

"Stay right there, Sami," she told me. "I've got to figure this out." Of course I wasn't going anywhere. I just wished there was some way I could help her.

I watched as Jasper, with difficulty, hoisted herself into an upright, sitting position. Then with one hand, she unbuttoned her outer shirt and pulled it free from her arms. Gingerly, she crooked her left elbow and pinned it to her side, like a bird with a broken wing, then wrapped the shirt around her elbow and forearm and tied its sleeves around her neck. It was awkward and took her a long time. When she was done, she closed her eyes and rested a little.

Next Jasper attempted to stand. She tried leaning forward and pushing up on her good hand, but that didn't work. She tried pushing with her legs only, backing up the rock, but that, too, was a failure. I was beginning to get seriously worried when finally she found a hand-hold in the rock behind her and half-pushed, half-dragged herself onto her feet. She yelped, favoring one foot. Something had gone wrong there, too. At least she was up. With foals, that was the essential thing, and I suspected it was the same for humans. I remembered vaguely what it felt like to try to manage my own un-ruly limbs, in my first attempt to stand after birth. But I hadn't been injured like Jasper. I thought she had done very well indeed. I suddenly felt intensely proud that she was mine.

Now came the part I could help with. Jasper hobbled over to retrieve her backpack, snagged in the brambles of a bush. She slung it over her good arm, then made her way slowly to my side. It was so good to feel her hands, to feel her weight leaning against my shoulder. She wrapped her arm around my neck and held me close for a long moment. It was also very nice when she found another carrot in her backpack and we shared it. Then, her right hand on my mane for support, Jasper and I limped down to the river.

· · ·

NEVER HAD WATER TASTED SO DELICIOUS AS that unknown bend of the river. Jasper and I drank and drank, then she started pouring handfuls of water over my face, my back, my poll. My coat felt filthy, itchy, and smelly with smoke. I appreciated Jasper's efforts, but I needed a real rinse. I sank to my knees, and Jasper shuffled out of the way, laughing, as I lay on my side with a grateful sigh and let the river's light current run over my body.

I hadn't thought that I was very damaged from the

fire, except for soreness and the lingering irritation from the smoke, until Jasper gave a gasp as I shook the river water from my coat.

"Sami, your tail!"

I flicked it and immediately felt what she saw. It only barely reached my hindquarters, even with a good swish. This was going to be seriously annoying. I doubted that the fly spray had made it with us on our flight.

"I hope it grows back," Jasper said, running her fingers through my now quite undignified, frizzled hair. So did I. An Arabian's tail should be a long, sweeping flag, streaming out behind us as we run, like light trailing a comet. (In addition to serving many practical purposes, of course.) True, I'd known a few grays and chestnuts in my mother's herd who had rather thin, wispy excuses for tails—but I did not want to join their ranks.

Jasper then proceeded to check every inch of me, running her hand down my legs, picking up my hooves, and inspecting me minutely for cuts and scrapes. There were a few, but they were small. I hadn't been burned, except for my tail, and neither had she, that I could tell. We shared another carrot, and I got a mouthful of grass from the banks, but there wasn't much. It was time to start home. The question was, Which direction? I didn't know if Jasper had any ideas on the subject, but I myself had only a vague sensation that east must be the answer, and that the river headed east. Jasper had washed her face and soaked her head in the river, and now she was attempting to get her hair into a ponytail single-handed. She managed a kind of snarled knob on the back of her head, then limped over to where I was grazing.

"So, which way, Sami? Which way should we go?" She looked to the sky, and up the trail we had just come down.

I started walking forward, along the riverbank. She grabbed hold of my mane again and followed.

"Whatever you say, girl," she told me.

.   .   .

IT DIDN'T TAKE US VERY LONG TO REALIZE that if we wanted to get anywhere quickly, it wasn't going to be with Jasper walking. She had lost a boot, but more than that, one of her legs was injured, and it quickly proved too weak to hold much weight over a distance. Her face was white though sweat streamed down her forehead, and then she stumbled badly, falling on her knees in the water. The solution was obvious to me, but Jasper seemed completely overwhelmed by what I did. I simply got down on my knees next to her, so she could easily get on my back. It was a trick I had learned years ago, in one of our fancy riding games.

"Sami?" My companion looked at me with wonder in her eyes.

Come on! I thought.

"There has never been anyone like you, Sami," she said in a quiet voice, stroking my muzzle. "You've saved me twice." And finally she managed to swing her bad leg over my back, picked up the reins, and I rose to my feet.

At first, the river was an ideal trail to follow, wide and placid, with enough vegetation on the banks for me to nibble periodically, and of course plenty of water for both of us. But I began to sense that it was turning, and in the wrong direction. It was also narrowing, and the banks to our right steepened, becoming rockier and even sheer in places, like the red cliffs on the opposite shore. I slowed my pace and looked ahead, sniffing the wind. I pawed one hoof indecisively, then turned and headed back downstream, searching for a trail. Jasper didn't question me. Her hands were slack on the reins and she was very quiet; so quiet and slumped in her seat that it worried me. Finally I picked out a path among the rocks, steeper than the one we came down, but not, I thought, impossible.

I needed every bit of my surefootedness during that climb, and every bit of my wits to determine where to place my hooves, which rocks would hold weight, which direction of a forking trail to follow. Slowly, my flanks heaving with effort, I pulled us from one part of the cliff to another. Jasper kept her weight forward, her hands wrapped tightly in my mane, and she did her best to follow my movements as I scrambled up loose, graveled dirt and fought for footing among the crags. At times I had to practically jump straight up, and my hind legs shook badly. Foam lathered at the corners of my mouth, and my labored breathing was loud and rough. Jasper's weight—well, of course it was fine. But awkward. And heavy to carry at such an angle. But I was strong, I was agile. I was Sami, Arabian mare. Climber of cliffs. I outran fire.

Still, I was more winded than I've ever been when we finally reached the top. Jasper started to swing her leg over, knowing how tired I was, but I just kept walking. We would need water, and we'd find it faster with Jasper aboard. My breathing was rapid and shallow, and my heart pounded like thunder. But I had more than enough left inside to keep going. In fact, I felt better with every step. I flicked my miserable stump of a tail and pricked my ears again. Time to look about me.

It was an unfamiliar landscape. Our westward run had taken us into a red, dusty, rocky scrubland. No wonder the fire hadn't reached here: There was nothing to burn. I decided to continue east and let the river catch up to us. I was almost certain it was *our* river, but there was no point in following all of its twists and turns if they took us out of the way of the direct route home. At least, what I hoped was the direct route.

The sun beat down and the air shimmered with heat. Like Jasper, I had lost a shoe somewhere in the cliffs, and a number of small rocks were wedged in my hooves. An eagle screamed from in the canyon below, leaving an echo behind. The silence seemed even larger afterward. I walked on.

"Let's find water." Jasper's voice was a faint rasp behind me. "I'm not feeling great, Sami. All I've got in this damn backpack is carrots and clothes. And a flashlight. That's helpful." It sounded as if she were trying to laugh, but I wasn't sure.

Yes, water. I needed it, too. Not urgently, but soon.

I walked on. And on.

. . .

THE SUN CAST LONG SHADOWS BEFORE US when I finally found a place to rest, a muddy stream purling down the mountainside to the river below. It wasn't lush and clear and flower filled as our streams and their banks were, but there was shade from a lone cottonwood tree and I could find things to eat on the slope.

Jasper didn't so much dismount as fall off my back, hitting her bad leg and crumpling to the ground with a groan. I nuzzled her hair and neck and nickered to her. She dragged herself over to the stream and we both plunged our heads in.

"Dad's going to kill me for drinking all this untreated water," Jasper said, and she gave the sort-of laugh again. "Okay, Sami, let's get you fixed up." It seemed to me that Jasper needed a lot more fixing up than I did, but I was grateful when she gave me carrots from the bag. Then she half-dragged, half-scooted herself over to the cottonwood, located a stick, and scooted back to me, until she was practically under my belly.

"You've never kicked me in your life, girl. Don't start now."

And Jasper raised my right foreleg, rested my hoof on her good knee, and went to work one-handed on the rocks in my hooves. It took her a long time to do all four, and she was exhausted afterward. I nibbled at her hair and chewed a bit on her shirt, which made her laugh. It was all I could do in return. My companion crawled over to the base of the tree and collapsed on her back, just managing to pull her pack over as a head-rest before she was asleep.

I kept vigil by her side. I watched the evening star rise. I watched over Jasper in the dark, under the meadow of stars.

. . .

WE WERE WOKEN BY THE SOUND OF COYOTE, keening to the summer moon. It was a weird, lonesome noise, and I shifted my weight restlessly. Jasper struggled to sit up, rubbing her eyes.

"Sami?" she croaked.

I snorted to let her know I was near. She was soon unconscious again, but for the rest of the night her sleep was disturbed. She cried out, sometimes for her mother and father, sometimes for me. Her scent was heavy with sweat, and with something else—illness. Fever.

Morning came, and still Jasper lay under the tree,

her eyes closed and her small face startlingly pale under its freckles. A terrible fear gripped me. *What if she did not wake?*

I nudged Jasper's neck with my muzzle and breathed over her face. I nudged her harder and she groaned.

Jasper. I stared at her, concentrating, then lipped her hair. *Wake up, Jasper. We have to go home.* She seemed to whisper something, but her eyes did not open.

I decided to drink and then try again. My wet, dripping muzzle turned out to be much more effective. Her eyes flickered open and her mouth almost formed a smile. It was a very slow process, but my sick foal, my Jasper, my companion, sat up, gave me another carrot, and pulled herself to her feet, using my leg, then my mane for support. She leaned her upper body across my back, legs dangling, and inch by inch, pulled herself up, breathing hard. It took several tries to swing her trembling leg over, but she finally managed it. Relief was a sweet cool river. We were on our way again. But I knew I could not let Jasper fall, and we could not stop again. I feared the scent of fever on her, and I feared her sleep. I did not think she would be able to get up again. And so I took every care not to stumble, to keep my stride even and steady, to take the least challenging path that still led east. Jasper tied the reins in a knot around her fist, then grabbed a tight hold on my mane, but as the morning wore on, she slumped forward, her forehead pressing against my crest. Her strength was fading, but she held on.

I myself was not in peak form, but I had discovered another horse within me. No, not *another* horse, but a deeper level within my blood, a reservoir I had never called on before, so I hadn't known existed. As I walked slowly between the *beyond* mountain and the red canyonland, I thought of my ancestors' treks through desert sands, through the fields of battle, through sandstorm, rainstorm, drought. I was one more Arabian mare, fortune bound in my forelock, trekking through history.

. . .

SCORCHED GRASS. BLACKENED TREES, TWISTED like cruel whips against the lowering sky. It looked like rain, and this burnt earth cried out for it. We had made it back to the fire-struck land, and it was a fearful sight. Smoke lingered on the mountainside, a bitter fog that set my nostrils tingling again. The ground was still hot in places, and I picked my way forward with great care. I was tiring, but I had to go on. Black earth, wisps of smoke, then a faint smell of rain. A rumble above, in the heavy clouds. I was tired, very tired. I felt the first drops of rain hit my coat, and then a few more. Jasper didn't stir. She had slid down so her arms were wrapped around my neck, her head resting against my shoulder. Her legs dangled from my sides, and I knew that a false step could unseat her. Slowly, I placed one hoof, then another, then another . . . blind to all except the feeling of east, of home. My head bowed as the rain came down and the charred trees and the brown smoke disappeared in floods of water that tumbled down on our backs. Water streamed into my eyes, my nostrils. My head sank lower and I stared at the ground before me. *One hoof, then another, then another . . .*

"SA-A-A-M-I-I-I! SAMI GIRL! HANG ON THERE, FILLY! I'M COMING!"

I raised my muzzle, confused. A whinny piercing the rain, cutting through the thunder. Then another:

"SAMI! WE SEE YOU!"

Surely that wasn't Magpie's voice? And Chief?

"COME TO ME, MARE!"

That couldn't be anyone but Buck.

I tried to neigh, and my voice broke. I lifted my muzzle higher and tried again.

"CHIEF! MAGPIE! BUCK!"

This time the triumphant voices of horses were joined by human shouts, by Red and Miz M and Peach. I stopped, bracing myself to scream out to them:

"HERE WE ARE! HERE WE ARE!"

The cavalry had arrived.

. . .

RED CRIED AS HE CUT MY MANE FREE FROM Jasper's fingers and lifted her gently from my back. He held her like a kitten curled against his chest, and he and Miz M pressed their faces into her tangled hair, sobbing. Everyone was crying, even Peach. I stood in the rain, my head close to Magpie's and Chief's, breathing in their familiar, comforting scents. Buck stood sentry before us.

Red transferred Jasper into Peach's arms, swung up on Magpie, then Peach very carefully handed Jasper up to him. She looked so small, so young, bundled in her father's arms with her head nestled under his chin. And suddenly my back felt very empty, and I was frightened. I took a step toward her and stumbled, almost falling to my knees.

"Sami?" Jasper could only whisper my name, but I heard her, through the rain, over her parents' voices. I would always hear her. I raised my muzzle and nickered anxiously. Then Miz M's arms were around me and she was crying into my mane. And Peach's arms were there, too. Jasper reached her hand down to stroke my muzzle.

"She saved my life," she whispered.

"We know," her family replied. "We know."

EPILOGUE

—————

THE EFFECTS OF THAT FIRE WERE FAR-reaching—in some ways, the blaze consumed Cold Creek Ranch as surely as it had burned our mountain. Started by a lightning strike, the course of events set in motion by the flames ended, improbably, at the doorstep of Mr. Sun's daughter, Emily.

I have a clear memory of walking back to the ranch, ponied behind Chief, my eyes fixed on Jasper's one bare foot dangling over Magpie's flank. I was so tired I didn't know if I could make the distance between the outlaws' cave and home—a distance Jasper and I had covered with wings only a few days before. Days that felt like years. But I kept my eyes on that small dirty foot, placed one hoof in front of the other, and eventually I looked up and we were home.

I remember seeing the black, ashy wreckage where the western side of the fence had been burned away by the flames, looking out over the bleak, charred pastureland, so many acres of kindling. But there the fire stopped, blocked by the river and the twin creeks that gave the ranch its name. The buildings—house, barn, and cabins—and about a quarter of the pasture had been spared the ravages of the flames.

After that, I don't remember very much, not for a while.

I know I was treated for smoke inhalation, and that treatment was often uncomfortable. I know that I burned the frog of the hoof where I lost my shoe and it took some time for that to heal. But the worst thing about that hazy, medicine-drowsy time was the sense of being severed from Jasper. I missed her weight.

She is my next clear memory: her face, wreathed in smiles, appearing like a small sun rising above my stall door. I whinnied my joy and she gave me a carrot, tip up. We went for a long, slow walk, staying close to the house, joined at various times by Peach, who brought her water, and Miz M, who kissed us both, and Red, who gave a halfhearted lecture about "taking it easy." Jasper's foot was encased in a thick white boot, and she walked with a sort of hop, balancing herself on one of Mr. Sun's canes. Mr. Sun came out to see us, too, and when we stopped to rest, he used his tools to decorate Jasper's new white boot. I'm not positive, but I think he might have painted me.

· · ·

WE DID LOSE THE RANCH, BUT WE GAINED SO
much more. I think the fire showed Jasper where her real
home was, with her family, and showed her parents that
no matter what, we had to be together. And so when
Mr. Sun called his daughter and asked if she still needed
a manager for her small horse ranch and training center, I think we were all ready to say yes.

We moved to the outskirts of a medium-size city.
The Munks' house was down the road from Emily Sun's.
We all had new jobs: Red ran the barn and helped train
young horses; Miz M started school (which I gathered
was not exactly like Jasper's, but involved learning things
about food–though I would have said Miz M knew
quite a bit already). Peach worked for another ranch, the
Flying Goose, but he came to visit Chief–and us–on the
weekends. Chief and Magpie and Buck helped keep
order in Emily's often tumultuous herd, but they de-
ferred to me. They had to–I had become lead mare. It
was one of the many roles I would play in my life–
endurance riding champion and dam of two fine colts
being another significant two–and it was very satisfying.

Even that was now long ago–twenty years, to be
precise. Yesterday I felt the weight of Jasper's daughter
on my back for the first time. She is only a baby, but I
will be here when she is old enough to hold the reins.

Until then, her mother will hold her on the front of my saddle, and the three of us will walk our world together. It is a good world—and a world not too many miles away from Cold Creek, now a wilderness. Jasper and her husband watch the birds and the changes in the land and teach people about them. *Conservation,* they call it, and I like the word, for to me it means conserving life. And when we're having an untrained day, Jasper will sneak out of the house at dawn, leaving the baby with her father, and the two of us will fly into the morning, into our world.

AUTHOR'S NOTE

THERE IS PERHAPS NO MORE STORIED BREED of horse than the Arabian, and their rich heritage could serve up plots for countless books of adventure. Marguerite Henry has probably written the best of them—*King of the Wind*—and, of course, Walter Farley's legendary Black Stallion was an Arabian, too. But I took much of my inspiration for Sami's character from older stories and nonfiction histories of the breed. In particular, I am indebted to George H. Conn's marvelous compendium, *The Arabian Horse in Fact, Fantasy, and Fiction* (1959), and to the endlessly interesting and authoritative history of the Egyptian Arab, *The Classic Arabian Horse* by Judith Forbis (1976).

Cold Creek Ranch in the story was similarly inspired by history—the history of the American West—and is loosely based on the long-defunct Jarvie Ranch, located on the Green River in Browns Park, Utah. I spent many hours wandering the beautiful wilds of this dramatic part of the country, and visited many nooks and crannies of the Outlaw Trail. At least, in my mind.

ANNIE WEDEKIND grew up riding horses in Louisville, Kentucky. Since then, she's been in the saddle in every place she's lived, from Rhode Island to New Orleans, South Africa to New York. Her first novel for young readers, *A Horse of Her Own,* was praised by *Kirkus Reviews* as "possibly the most honest horse book since *National Velvet* . . . A champion." She lives with her family in Brooklyn, New York. www.anniewedekind.com